dark storm clouds

break of dawn

golden shafts of light

shadows of the future

the party

It was already approaching nine o'clock in the evening and the excruciating trial by ordeal that he was about to face hung like a spectre over his shattered soul. Before he left his penthouse he paused in front of the large, full-length mirror alongside the walnut-clad elevator doors. He stared into the hollowness of his dark eyes and his image stared a steady, unyielding stare back. He was a handsome, mid-twenties, rich widower who was sun-stained by endless walks along Cornish cliffs, the beauty of which helped keep the ugliness of his memories at bay. His striking looks, his wealth and the vulnerability, which he wore like a second skin, made him prey to women wherever he went. Women he would normally take extreme caution to avoid at all cost but who today were going to encircle him. Going to a party in an exclusive London residence, which would be infested by the London fashionista, was destined to push him beyond his very limited emotional capacity and into the shadowy, dark places which he carried around buried in the recesses of his tortured mind. He stared at his image looking back at him and willed the universe to transport him back to his Cornish cottage where he lived in glorious isolation and where the pain inflicted by other mortals could not touch him. Cornwall was safe - the party in London was not.

As Dorus descended from his penthouse in the almost silent, private, brass and mirror-lined elevator he closed his eyes to embrace the last vestiges of his solitude. He unplugged his hybrid Audi from its electrical docking station alongside the elevator doors and climbed in. The garage doors slid aside on command revealing a rush of motorised bustle and he reluctantly emerged into the street to do battle with the traffic in London's upmarket St Katharine Docks area. The rain was falling vertically and relentlessly as though a black cloud had settled above him and was reluctant to move. The darkness of the night and the misery of the rain compounded the darkness and misery in his soul. The almost inaudible sound of the electric power of the hybrid car was easily subsumed by the snare drum rattle of the rain on the car roof, the hiss of the tyres slicing their way through the standing water and the swish of the windscreen wipers repeating their inexorable torment like a demonic metronome. He flicked the radio on in order to listen to Classic FM in an attempt to drown out his growing foreboding as he wove his way along the forty-minute drive through the dark, sodden London streets towards Ruth's exclusive Fitzrovia townhouse. He did not want to go to her party and she knew he didn't want to go to her party but she had insisted and Dorus was powerless to resist her. Ruth was perhaps the only person in his limited circle of acquaintances that he trusted. Ruth was a friend. Ruth was his only friend. As an incentive, she had reserved one of the two parking spaces right outside her front door so that he might park alongside her Porsche Panamera and then have no option but to enter. On arriving, he remained sitting in his car listening to the hypnotic rattle of the rain and to Classic FM which failed to penetrate his angst until the digital display on the dashboard indicated it was 10 o'clock and time to face a houseful of people he didn't know nor want to know.

He stepped out of his car with his head bowed from the rain and met another body simultaneously arriving. He deduced it was a woman but, with her coat over her head as a makeshift umbrella, it was hard to tell. Something in the half-hidden stranger's gait indicated the unknown person might not be a threat. Standing side by side, he pressed the doorbell and the heavy, half glazed wooden door swung open almost instantly emitting a rush of heat, sound and expensive fragrance. Ruth stood in the gateway and raised her arms and her voice as she whooped with joy and stepped forwards to hug both visitors in tandem before realising the folly of her largesse given the inclemency of the weather. Instead, she pulled them both in through the portal still whooping and screeching until all three stood in the vaulted hallway of an extravagantly designed interior.

"You came! You both came! I can hardly believe it! Dorus, Anaya, I take it you have both met."

She gestured to Dorus' rain-stained doorstep companion to indicate that an introduction was momentarily being offered.

Before either had a chance to explain their mutual acquaintance had only occurred seconds before and had not fully included having actually *met*, they were both tugged deeper into the melee of bodies, the cacophony of overly animated conversations and the odour of fashionable perfumes.

"Anaya, put your coat over there. Dorus come on in – let me introduce you to Brian and Dotty. They are just so adorable. I've been telling them all about you. They can't wait to meet you."

Brian and Dotty dutifully stepped half a pace aside to allow room for Dorus to intrude, unwelcomed into what had been their private space. Their facilitations were warm but their eyes betrayed the fact that they did not welcome the unknown intruder into their world which hitherto had been masking a barely concealed coquetry. Introductions over, Ruth disappeared into the crowd as if by illusion and Dorus was lost, alone, exposed and panicking. His conversation with Brian and Dotty lasted approximately ninety seconds before he made excuses and moved on – moved away to find solitude. The same conversation tortured him over and over again as he was repeatedly interrupted whilst he made his way from the palatial living room to the basement kitchen to collect a wine glass of grape juice behind which he could temporarily shelter.

Returning to the crowded living room, the sound wall intensified and became dense like an impenetrable jungle. He could no longer distinguish words from the solid noise enveloping him. He felt his heart faulter and panic claw at his ribs. He noticed and avoided Anaya at intervals before he found his way to the patio doors and escaped out into the garden where he stood, sheltered from the rain, on the covered veranda. He settled for an instant alongside a small but animated group of smokers and vapers who had found comradery in their nicotine addiction. Waiting his moment to assure none of the cloud-engulfed addicts had acknowledged him, he made his escape down the winding, slate pathway to the open fronted summer house he knew would be his sanctuary until he could find an unnoticed escape back into the anonymity of the streets and then on to the safety of his penthouse. Once inside, he slumped back, closed his eyes and listened to the world he had found himself inhabiting that evening. He listened to the relentless pounding of the rain, the now muffled quagmire of party sound and the bursts of amplified conversations as smokers opened and closed the patio door to retreat from or to gain access to their addiction den.

Having drunk his grape juice, he now slid the wineglass out into the rain and let the deluge refill his glass with London infused rainwater.

An indeterminate length of time passed and then his eyes flicked open and his heart pounded momentarily as he subconsciously monitored the sound of a door opening and closing imperceptibly longer than had become routine. Smokers rushed in and out but now someone had emerged into the garden area with other intentions. Believing he was still safe in his recluse he relaxed again but then a new threat presented itself and froze still as it entered the summer house and spoke involuntarily.

"Oh, shit. I thought no-one would be here."

Dorus immediately recognised her as his doorstep companion, Anaya, and he summoned words of politeness.

"Don't worry. Come in. It's pouring. Unless you're after a fag; then the smokers are all up there."

"I didn't mean to disturb you. No, I don't smoke. Sorry, I should go."

"No, come and join me. We can be refugees together for a bit. You are Anne… Anne… er. I think we arrived together. Annie, isn't it?"

"Anaya actually. No-one calls me Annie, but actually I rather like it, so you can call me Annie if you like - and what's your name? Dorian, was it?"

"No, Dorus."

"That's unusual."

"It's Dutch. Not that I'm Dutch. I think my parents had a sense of humour. Maybe it was because they spent most of their courtship smoking marijuana in cafés in Amsterdam. It's bugged me all my life. Half the time people call me Dorian or worse still I get called Doris."

"OK. I promise not to call you Doris. So Dorus, what brings you to Ruth's salubrious summerhouse on this lovely evening?"

"Oh, fear mostly. I'm hiding until I can go home. How early do you think it might be possible to leave a party without insulting the hostess?"

Anaya laughed without offering a solution.

"What makes you think I'd know party etiquette?"

"Well, you seemed totally at home in there. You looked pretty popular to me."

"What do you mean?"

"I was watching. I mean I was people watching. Not just watching you – that would be weird. I reckon guys were hitting on you about every two minutes and you seemed to know just how to swat them off like flies. Half of them were married or with partners too, I reckon."

"That's about right I'm afraid. A single gal can't go to a party without the vultures circling."

"Firstly, may I apologise on behalf of my species and secondly may I reassure you that this is a hit-free-zone. I am incapable of hitting on anyone so you are officially safe here."

Stifling back her curiosity as to why Dorus might want to volunteer so early in their meeting the information that he was incapable of hitting on anyone, she pushed the conversation onwards to what she hoped would find safer ground.

"Glad to hear it. I'm not in a place in my life to be hit on either. So, let's agree to be on neutral ground. I don't actually hate all men, just very nearly all of them."

"Fair enough. Me too. And can I add hating most women to the list just for good measure?"

"If you must. Anyway, so, we are in neutral territory. A mutual safety zone."

"Weird when you say it out loud, but yes."

Having established a safety zone in which they could temporarily reside at least on a superficial, social level, Anaya continued.

"I take it you know Ruth."

"Yup. Through my – er – er – er – my late wife. They were at St Paul's Girls' School together." Then, after a poignant pause deliberately designed to exacerbate his new acquaintance's sudden awkwardness, he continued. "Did you see how I just killed the conversation with that 'late wife' comment I slipped in? I should warn you. I am boring, socially awkward and conversationally retarded. So good luck. You might want to make your escape now whilst you can. I shan't be offended. Most people give me a wide berth."

"Er, I must admit, learning that you are a widower in the first couple of minutes of talking to you has stumped me a bit. I'm so sorry for your loss …"

"Don't be. Let's move on quickly and try another line of conversation before it gets too embarrassing."

"OK. Good plan. This is an easy one. A standard party intro question." Anaya inhaled deeply to denote a fresh start in the conversation. "So, Dorus, what do you do for a living?"

"You'll regret asking that."

"Why? I thought I was on safe ground there. It's a standard party ice breaker."

"I'll give it ninety seconds before it grinds to a standstill. This is the same conversation I had ten times in there before I escaped. Go on, ask me again."

Despite Anaya now beginning to regret her decision not to have escaped from Dorus when she had the chance, she repeated the question obediently.

"OK. So, Dorus, what do you do for a living?"

"I'm a musician."

With some relief that what appeared to be an interesting vein of conversation had emerged, she continued.

"Oh, that's great. What do you play?"

"I write."

"That's cool. What kind of music? Classical?"

"No. Pop music."

"Brilliant. Would I know any of your songs?"

"Almost certainly. Lots of them. They are all over the radio all day, every day. I hardly dare turn the radio on unless it's for classical music."

"Wow. Like what? Give me some examples?"

"I can't tell you."

"What?"

"I'm not allowed to tell you."

"What?"

"I'm a ghost writer and I'm covered in non-disclosure agreements - NDAs. The NDAs make me keep it a secret that I write the songs that famous pop stars claim to be their own."

Anaya paused hoping to find a suitable response before Dorus smiled and broke the tense silence with a laugh.

"Ninety seconds about right? Maybe a bit less. Look, it's not as bad as it sounds. I write the songs but then I meet up with a client in London in a godawful penthouse and we jam our way through them until the songs stop being mine and slowly become theirs. Then they pay me shed loads of money and I then get truckloads of royalties when they go platinum with *their* songs. The fact is, they are so busy touring and doing TV interviews that they just don't have the creative capacity to keep churning out new stuff. So, I do it for them. As far as I'm concerned, they do all the hard work what with all the gigs and media attention and then I get most of the money. Anyway, now it's your turn. Annie, what do you do for a living?"

"I'm an architect."

"Wow. Genuinely, wow. You have no idea how much respect I have for you guys. You design and build amazing buildings – which somehow don't fall down – and then people live their lives, their dramas, their loves, their failures and their successes in them. Some of the great buildings don't just define society, they create it. Who do you work for?"

"Yasha and Partners. One of the biggest and most prestigious practices in London."

"Good for you."

"Well, I did until today. I got sacked today."

"What?"

"See, I can kill a conversation too."

"Yup. That worked well as a conversation stopper. Go on then, what the hell happened?"

"To be more accurate, I was 'let go' today, not sacked. Me and two others were taken on as new graduates to work on a big new design. We were all on one-year contracts getting paid not much more than the living wage. We are supposed be grateful for being given the opportunity. Interns, really. We did a damn good job too, but they pitched the design to the client earlier this week and we didn't get the contract. So, we are no longer needed. I packed my bag and left today. The other two got re-tasked onto other projects. To be blunt, my line manager said I could move to another project too – if I slept with him – so I packed my bag instead and walked out. I now get paid for two months but I have no work. So, I'm looking for another job."

"That's outrageous! I hope you reported him. And I hope they gave you tons of redundancy."

"No point reporting him. My word against his. Besides, I need a reference so stirring up shit wouldn't help that. And no redundancy – fixed term contract. It's all a bit mercenary."

"I'm outraged! So, let's move on. OK, so what's your next job?"

"I'm looking. Problem is, the economy is on a downer right now which means big builds are all on hold and so architects are getting laid off. There's not much about right now."

"What happens in two months if you don't get a new job, then?"

"I can't think about it yet. Out on the streets I guess if I can't pay my rent."

"And there was I, arrogantly going on about making shed loads of cash for writing crappy, throwaway pop songs whilst you are being turned out onto the streets as an amazingly well qualified architect. I feel so stupid now. Believe it or not, I am desperate for an architect. Not the glamorous work you are used to but an interesting project nonetheless I think."

"For the penthouse you just described as being godawful?"

"Good God no! That is past saving. It is just awful. It looks like some sort of dystopian film set. I just use it when I meet clients. No, I live in Cornwall. I have an old stone cottage overlooking the sea. It is a bit of a mystery house. That's my home, but I do also have a small cottage in Provence which I think of as my spiritual home. I'll be going there to chop wood and restore my soul after enduring London. I only come to London when I have to meet a client."

"Wow. I've never been to Cornwall let alone France."

"What? You are kidding me. Everyone's been to Cornwall. It sometimes feels like everyone is actually *in* Cornwall every summer."

"No, not joking. So, the Cornish house needs some *tlc*?"

"Yup. It has got itself really confused. I bought it as a wreck and had it done up but it then got all weird. I need an inspired architect to sort it out. If you've never been to Cornwall, maybe you should have a working holiday and see if you can suss out the problem for me."

"Well, you never know. If I can't find another job, I might just take you up on that offer. You should be careful what you say at parties just in case people you meet sheltering from the rain in summer houses think you mean it."

"I do mean it. But, what about you? Where are you from? I can't detect an accent but I'm guessing you are a Londoner. You seem like a town-gal."

"Spot on. London born and bred. I live in a house-share in Islington."

"Ah, I don't know London that well, but I know Islington a bit. Really nice area. I've walked along a canal there and had a pint in a pub right alongside the water. I remember nearly being killed by joggers and cyclists who don't seem to think walkers have any right to be there. I was on my way to the King's Place for a concert."

"That sounds like it. I live in a house-share with five others. I rent a tiny room in a big Victorian terrace. They are all professionals like me, but they are all party-mad-coke-heads, so I tend to bury my head in my work to avoid them - or at least I did until today. Now I don't have any work. So that's a bit awkward now."

"So, if I've got this right, you don't want to stay at the party and get hit on all night and you don't want to go back to your party-mad-coke-head housemates. If you don't mind me asking, how does an attractive girl who doesn't want to get hit on get home anyway? I mean, get home safely to Islington from Fitzrovia in the early hours of the morning?"

"I don't. Ruth has offered me a room for the night."

"Oh, I see. So, you have to go back into the party and get hit on all through the night by increasingly drunk partygoers until the last person falls over or leaves."

"Yup. I guess so. You have grasped the very essence of my shit life there, Dorus. Thanks for rubbing it in. I'm dreading it. At least you can escape."

"Look. I know this will sound weird, but why not bail and come back to the penthouse. It's at the top of a tower block called Katharine Heights right by St Katharine Docks. It's actually on two floors. There is an open-plan living area and then there is a sleeping level below that. Honestly, it is like a Holiday Inn. There are six en-suite bedrooms all with hotel style locks. You can lock yourself in and have as much privacy as you want. It is all geared up for five-star guest accommodation – the music business is very needy."

Anaya eyed Dorus cautiously wondering how to politely decline his offer before he sensed her discomfort and continued.

"I know it might look like this weirdo stranger you have only just met at a party has just asked you back to his place but, I promise, it is a genuine offer. It's up to you."

"I must admit that it sounds tempting. I've always wanted to see inside that block. It's quite famous in architectural circles. But I don't know. My mum always told me not to go off with complete strangers back to their penthouses in London in the middle of the night."

"She is a wise woman. But, how come Katharine Heights is famous?"

"It's always put forward as an example of venture capital building. Apparently, a bunch of venture capitalists stumped up the money to build it cheap. They just left it empty. Not even finished inside. But the new building triggered gentrification of the whole area. Now it's one of the most expensive areas in London and the value of their tower block went through the roof. The venture capitalists, or *vulture* capitalists as I like to call them, sold up and made millions without anyone ever having actually lived there. Both kind of clever and kind of immoral, really."

Before further consideration of Dorus' offer could take place, a burst of sonance overlayered with Ruth's vocal remonstrations hurled itself out of the party and into the garden like a human canon ball.

"Where's that no-good husband of mine? Having a sneaky fag? Derek? You out here? I bet he's hiding from me. You'd better not be hiding in the summerhouse with that Patricia woman."

Sounds of Ruth approached the summer house refugees until she burst into their space like a genie released from a lamp after hundreds of years containment. Ruth barely drew breath before words fell out of her like a waterfall bursting from a newly formed spring.

"Dorus! Anaya! You are here. I can't tell you how happy I am you two came. I know you are not into parties, so I am truly blessed you came. And yes, before you ask me you are allowed to leave at any time. You just came. That's all that matters. Well, Dorus, you can go but Anaya, you are staying here, so you can't."

Dorus found a small aperture in Ruth's hagiographical monologue.

"Actually, I just suggested Anaya could come back to the penthouse to crash if she wanted."

Ruth barely inhaled again.

"Oh my God, Anaya! You got an invite to Faulty Towers. Just go, darling. It's amazing. He never invites anyone – unless they are about to offer him millions for his songs. Just go. Oh, and he is totally harmless so don't worry on that count. He'll look after you, not seduce you. He can't seduce anyone, poor thing – no offence Dorus."

"None taken."

She continued.

"Off you pop you two and don't leave it so long next time. Dorus, when are you off again? Can we catch up before you go? If you see my invisible husband, tell him I want him. People are asking for him. Apparently, some people actually want to talk to him – no accounting for taste."

Then, not waiting for responses, Ruth was gone into the rain and was subsumed back into the menagerie of the party.

"Well," Anaya spoke through a much-needed exhalation, "it looks like I'm going to the penthouse. Why does she call it Faulty Towers?"

"Oh, it's just that I'm always moaning about it. I pick fault with it all the time. I do know it is kind of, well, splendid, but it is just not me. Seriously, it is just a place for me to sleep. So, what's your verdict. Coming to Faulty Towers or staying here to be hit on by drunkards?"

"Such a tough choice when you put it like that. Right – decision made – Faulty Towers it is."

"So, if you are ready, shall we go?"

"I guess so. I just need to get my bag."

"I'll wait out front. My car is there. It'll only be about a thirty or forty minute drive."

"You are driving? But haven't you been drinking?"

"One glass of grape juice and one glass of rain water so far. So, I think I'm OK to drive."

"Oh, OK. Great. See you in a minute."

They made their way past the smokers, some of whom were passing marijuana scented joints between them, back to the party and across the living room where flamboyant, alcohol-influenced dancing hindered their passage making progress to their exit slow and precarious. Dorus made a dash through a gap in the solid wall of drunken flesh to the front door and to his escape without engaging any eyes and waited, sheltering from the relentless wetness. Moments later, Anaya appeared now wearing the coat she had previously used as an umbrella and carrying a small, canvas overnight bag. With no words offered, Dorus aimed his plip at the Audi which obediently blinked back to life signalling to Anaya to take the half dozen paces and to climb into the passenger seat. For the first time Dorus noted that Anaya was cursed with an understated beauty that made her stand out and beckoned for her to be the attention of male predators. He didn't recognise the origin of her name but could see she had dark, olive skin and even darker hair which made him wonder if she was of Asian descent.

Once underway and threading the car back to Faulty Towers, Dorus picked up the seed he had previously handed to Anaya.

"When we get there, perhaps I can show you some photos of my Cornish place so you can see the architectural problem."

"Yeah, that would be great."

"I don't want to put the fear of God into you, but I've actually already been through two architects. The first one quickly decided that the job was beyond her and left. I respect her for that. The second one charged me four and a half thousand quid to come up with a load of bollocks."

"No pressure then."

Dorus laughed and then turned his concentration away from small talk and back to trying to pick his way through the rain-stained windscreen whilst Anaya tried to pick her way through the awkward silence and her rising discomfort.

"If someone had told me I would be sitting in a car in the middle of the night heading to a penthouse with a complete stranger I would have laughed at them. I must be mad, but Ruth said it should be OK, so here I am."

"You just have to love Ruth, don't you? Love her and do what she tells you."

"Oh yes. Without doubt. I owe her so much. I would do anything for her. She got me through some tough times."

"Me too."

Both Dorus' and Anaya's minds retreated to their separate tragic pasts which were now united by the mutual inclusion of Ruth but which directed them to a dense silence broken only by the rattle of rain and by angry motorists releasing their frustrations through their car horns.

As they arrived at the threshold of Faulty Towers, a steel and glass folding garage door opened itself meticulously after Dorus had lowered his window and placed a hand on a biometric security pad and they entered an underground carpark marked out for a dozen cars.

"I expected there to be more parking spaces, Dorus."

"Oh, no. This is just the private car park for the penthouse."

"Of course. Silly me. The pop stars must have a private car park. They can't be mixing with ordinary folk like me."

Dorus attached his hybrid Audi to Faulty Towers by its umbilical cord and left it parked very precisely in one of the marked bays despite there being no other vehicle to necessitate the care he displayed. They walked to the elevator and he placed his hand on a second biometric security pad commanding the elevator doors to hiss obediently before they were whisked with effortless speed to the lofty luxury of Dorus' secret hermitage.

the penthouse

The elevator doors opened with balletic synchrony and ushered Anaya into a secret, aerial world. She stepped forwards followed by a silent and apprehensive Dorus. So few people had ever entered this veiled part of his being that he feared that Anaya's presence might feel like a trespass into the privacy of his anima. She walked to the epicentre of what was a curved, octagonal, open-plan room which gave a 360-degree vista of the City of London, St Pauls Cathedral and the River Thames. Anaya firstly stood still and then began a slow-motion gyration.

"Dorus. I'm not one for bad language, but this has to be an exception. This is fucking amazing!"

"Fucking awful, more like. Sorry, but maybe Ruth calls this place *Fawlty* Towers as in Basil Fawlty because I'm a miserable git."

"How can you say this is awful? It is just fabulous!"

Anaya continued her almost incorporeal rotation soaking in the interior layout of the open-plan penthouse; the luxurious kitchen at the centre with copper pans dangling like ornaments over the cooker surrounded by black marble preparation surfaces; the living and dining areas with suspended staircases leading both upwards and downwards and the panoramic architectural splendour of her home town.

Dorus interrupted her awe.

"First things first, Annie. Let's choose you a bedroom. You need your privacy."

His reference to her needing her privacy was intended to hide the fact that it was he that needed his.

Without waiting for a response, he set off down the extravagantly designed wooden and stainless-steel staircase with Anaya in an increasingly nervous pursuit until they reappeared in a single, long corridor along which Anaya quickly counted six identical, wooden doors. She had to stifle her rising panic as past memories began to trigger her psyche.

"This one is mine." Dorus banged on a door casually as they passed. "So, you can have any of the others. Here, try this one. I think the view is pretty cool from this one."

He pushed open a door at the other end of the corridor revealing an expansive bedroom complete with a view over the City of London and the River Thames.

"There's the bathroom. There should be the usual shampoos etcetera. You've got a telly and stuff. I think it is all pretty self-explanatory. Teas, coffees and so on are in the kitchen upstairs. Will this do you?"

"Oh, I think I'll manage. Honestly Dorus, this is all fantastic. It really is very kind of you to put me up."

"No worries. Let me grab your bag and bring it down and you can get settled in. I'm going to have a cup – or maybe a glass of something before I turn in. You are very welcome to join me or you can just head straight to bed if you want."

The casual tone in Dorus' voice assuaged Anaya's trepidation as she smiled, turned and drifted towards the expansive window beyond the super king-sized bed. Dorus left her standing at the thick, one-way, panoramic window taking in the London tableau and allowing her mounting tension to subside. He reappeared a few moments later with her bag and she span around to greet him with a smile.

"Actually, I could really do with a nightcap if that's OK? I feel like I need to offload a few tensions. I'm afraid the party wound me up a bit."

"Great, me too. Come on up when you are ready."

"Not to sound too keen for some alcohol, but I'm ready now if you are."

Dorus offered her a genuine smile and nodded in acceptance. They retraced their steps to the living area and Anaya paced around inquisitively taking in the finer design details of the luxury penthouse before locating and occupying the corner of an L-shaped sofa which suggested both comfort and safety to her. The depth of the cushions embraced her body and swaddled her mind.

"What do you fancy, Annie? I'm going to have a scotch, but I've got most things. Tea? Coffee? Wine? Something more serious?"

"I'll join you in a scotch, if that's OK? I don't really drink much, but I seem to be breaking all my rules tonight, so what the hell."

"Excellent."

Dorus picked out two heavy, cut glass whisky glasses and a decanter of Aberlour single malt whisky. Putting both glasses down on the table in front of Anaya he excised the stopper from the decanter and poured two good sized drams. He handed one to Anaya and then, sitting diametrically opposite to her on the sofa, he raised his glass and began a toast.

"Here's to …."

"Here's to our safety zone."

"Yes. I'll drink to that!"

They raised their glasses above their eyeline and then both gulped down a mouthful in unison exhaling with a gasp as the whisky hit the back of their throats. Dorus continued.

"Actually, let's drink to friendship in our safety zone."

"Yes. I like that. Cheers."

They each took a second swig and relaxed backwards and downwards into their respective, fatigued slumps allowing the softness of the upholstery to reassure them. Despite their increasing, mutual sense of ease with each other they held back their wish to share the source of their vestigial unease. Each were so accustomed to hiding their traumatic histories both from themselves and to others that they resisted the unfathomable urge to begin sharing their torment with their new and unfamiliar acquaintances despite a growing mutuality of trust.

Dorus found a sentence to break the sudden social impasse they had reached.

"Actually, Annie, I have to hand it to you."

"I find it funny you calling me Annie. Only my parents ever called me Annie. I like it. What do you mean *hand it to me*? What have I done?"

"I live the life of a hermit, avoiding all social contact and yet you have managed to hold me in conversation for ..." he checked the clock, "... about two hours! That takes some skill."

Anaya's nervous laugh gave way to a genuine, warm and disarming smile.

"No, I take my hat off to you. I avoid all fraternisation at all cost and yet here I am, in the middle of the night, in a penthouse with a complete stranger knocking back whisky. You certainly broke down my barriers!"

"Well, perhaps Ruth had a hand in it. She almost commanded us to trust each other and come back here. Anyway, shall I show you my house in Cornwall so you can decide if it's something you want to have a go at?"

"Brilliant. Yes, I'd love to see it."

Her acceptance of his offer felt more polite than genuine but showing her some images of his Cornish retreat would serve the purpose of both prolonging the conversation and diverting it away from more testing topics.

Dorus fetched his laptop from the edge of a polished, white grand piano at the far end of the living area and flicked it open causing it to obediently wake from its torpor. He tapped a few commands on the keys and Google Earth began zooming in from space to finally settle over a rugged Cornish cliff. Anaya leaned over to square up to the screen to demonstrate her interest.

"There she is. Home. All you can really see is the house, but I need to explain something. First of all, when I had it renovated about five years ago the builder said that although it looks like a nineteenth century cottage, the cuts on the stone blocks suggest it is much older. I mean, *a lot* older. Except, he told me the way it was built was definitely twentieth century. All very odd. Then, after I moved in, I decided to convert the cellar into a wine cellar. I thought it was odd having a cellar at all because it's built on solid granite, but there it was. So, I set to. But on the far wall of the cellar there was a hollow sound when I tried to put up the shelves. The hollow sound was door shaped, so I did what any self-respecting guy would do."

"You hit the wall with a sledge hammer?"

"Exactly. And sure enough, behind the plaster was a door. A great big cast iron door. The kind of door you see in bank vaults in cops-and-robbers movies. It took me another day and a half to prise it open, but behind it was a massive, manmade, concrete cavern. And I mean massive. To cut a long story short, firstly I got a surveyor in who pronounced it safe. In fact, he said it would withstand a nuclear bomb attack. In fact, his guess was that it was a giant air raid shelter. I've got my music studio down there now which is great. I can make as much noise as I like and not care about disturbing anyone. You can see the house is set back from

26

the cliff. Well, the bunker goes all the way from the house to the edge. It's enormous!"

"That's incredible. Did you ever find out what it is?"

"Yes, eventually. I wrote to the Ministry of Defence who denied all knowledge of it. Then, a couple of weeks later I got another letter from them saying they had since declassified it and so could now confirm it was one of a number of bunkers built in the second world war just in case Churchill and his war cabinet had to relocate from their war bunker in London. I think they were a bit embarrassed. The details had been misplaced apparently, but now I owned the land so I owned the bunker too."

"So, a massive cock-up in Cornwall, then?"

"Yes. A total bureaucratic cock-up. But look carefully. There's more. Look behind the house. It's hard to see because it is all overgrown."

Anaya leaned forwards to focus and now engaged genuine interest.

"Oh, my God. There is an archaeological feature there. I can just see the shadow of it."

"Spot on. I got the university archaeology department to take a look. They say the shape of it looks like it might be a mediaeval church, but they can't be sure because someone has built a bloody house on top of it!"

"So, are you saying that your house was built in the twentieth century but made to look like an old cottage and was actually built using stone robbed from a mediaeval church?"

"Whoa! You are good. It took me five years to come to that conclusion. Well, I can't be sure, but maybe. So, there is an odd house, a war bunker and an archaeological mystery. None of it sits comfortably. So, Anaya, if you want a challenge - solve the mystery and then come up with a grand design which will faithfully tell the story of the whole site. Quite a challenge. I'll pay the going rate for your services of course. I'm happy to just pay for a consultation even if you decide not to take the project on. Honestly, I really want to get my house sorted out, so meeting you at the party might be a happy coincidence."

Dorus looked up from the screen of the laptop to place his gaze firmly onto Anaya to denote that a challenge had been offered and that a response was required.

"I hope it's not just the whisky talking, but I'm really excited by what you just told me. You know, for the last 10 months I have been working on a big new sky scraper but all I ever did day after day was sit in front of a computer screen and work out stresses and suchlike to make sure it wouldn't fall down. Not very creative. But this - wow! This would be actually creative."

"I'm serious if you want to take look. I mean, if you see it and then don't want to do it, fair enough. But I'd love you to take a look. And I will pay the going rate for a consultation, obviously."

"I'm interested. Maybe we could talk about it tomorrow."

"Of course."

As the whisky loosened Anaya's reticence, she risked the question that had been burning at her tongue since they had met.

"Forgive me asking, Dorus - and don't think you have to answer - but did you say you live there on your own?"

"Yes. I've been there on my own since I bought it."

"Well, is losing your wife the reason you have decided to live alone? I mean, I can't think of a much more eligible bachelor than you. Good looking, famous, money. Sorry, am I getting too personal?"

Dorus emptied his whisky in one mouthful and poured another.

"Well, I'm not sure about the good-looking bit, and definitely not famous, but, OK, look, I really do want you to come and do some architectural magic in Cornwall, so I'm going to tell you what happened. That way you can decide to run a thousand miles from me if you want to. All I ask is that you don't say anything. OK?"

"Of course. I wouldn't dream of betraying a confidence."

"No, I mean don't say anything to me when I tell you. I find it hard to talk about. So, I'll tell you but just listen and don't say anything."

"OK, I promise."

Dorus gulped another slug of whisky as a visual indication he was summoning courage to share his dark secret.

"Help yourself to more whisky if you want."

In solidarity more than in preference, she did.

Dorus continued.

"I'll keep it short. I'll cut out all the gory details. The fact is, I fell in love with Charlotte – Charlie for short – at primary school. It was a classic childhood romance. We got married at eighteen much to the disapproval of both her parents and mine. It was very romantic. We eloped actually. All very corny when I look back on it. Soon after the wedding, my parents were killed in a car crash. I hadn't even had time to reconcile with them. I was quite a mess. Then about a year after we were married a friend took me aside and told me Charlie had been unfaithful. I mean really unfaithful. Lots of lovers apparently. All the way through our relationship up to and including our marriage. It destroyed me. I didn't know what to do. I should have walked, I know, but I didn't. She admitted it all when I challenged her, but she persuaded me to stay and I persuaded myself that we somehow still had a future together. It was really hard, but then, almost immediately, she got pregnant. That sealed it, so I tried to make a go of it. Nine months later she went into hospital and had a gorgeous little baby boy. Tragically, it transpired she had a congenital heart condition and she suffered a massive heart attack and died during labour. They had to do an emergency caesarean to get the baby out of her dead body. I ended up in a private room, in shock, grieving and holding my tiny, beautiful son – I called him Jack. Then, after a while a man appeared in the doorway together with a nurse. They just stood there looking at me. I thought he must be a doctor. He finally said that he had come to get his son. His words simply didn't compute. The nurse was trembling. She took Jack from me and said they would rush a DNA test through. Turns out, it wasn't my son. That guy had fucked Charlie and totally fucked me up. She had been sleeping with that guy and he was the father. I went into some sort of frontal lobe shock thing. The shrinks had a long name for it. My brain just switched off to protect me. To cut a long story short – six months of therapy later I was still a wreck. Eventually a psych taught me to pack all the pain away into a box and hide it. That seems to be working, but now I can't even think about having any relationships with anyone for fear of opening the box. So, I'm a hermit. When I am alone, no-one can hurt me."

The words 'when I'm alone, no-one can hurt me' hung in the air and drifted like swirling smoke between them until Anaya coughed out the words she had promised not to.

"Jesus! That's unbelievable. Just awful."

"You promised not to say anything – but I'll forgive you for that."

Anaya became mute. Dorus stared and then spoke.

"And you? Just because I spilled my guts out doesn't mean you have to, but I sensed something. I might be wrong, and you don't have to say anything, but ..."

"OK. I never talk about this, but something says I'm going to. Likewise, can you not comment afterwards. I'll tell you, but I'm not going to talk about it. OK?"

"OK."

"I was eighteen. In love with Rohan. In fact, it was my birthday. He had booked a hotel room and I was going to give him my virginity. We'd waited until I was eighteen. It was going to be the most romantic night of my life. We checked in and went up to the room. He said he would go out to buy condoms and leave me to undress and get into bed. I thought it was a bit odd he hadn't brought any with him considering there was only one thing on the agenda. About twenty minutes later he came back. But he was with three of his mates. In short, they held me down, gagged me, put a bag over my head and then each of them raped me in turn. I thought I was going to die. Actually, I wanted to die. One of them pushed a hole through the bag to let me breathe. When they finished, they just left. I lay there crying for hours. Then I had a shower for some reason and checked out. He hadn't even paid. I didn't tell anyone for a week. I was too ashamed. Eventually, I told Ruth and she persuaded me to go to the police. Apparently, I had left it too long. There was no evidence either in me or in the hotel room, so when the police interviewed them, they just denied it. There was no case."

"Holy shit!"

"Ah! No comment, remember. There's more. I told my parents after another week or so. In their culture, women who get raped shame the family. So, they upped sticks and went back to Lahore – just abandoned me. If it hadn't been for Ruth, I don't know what I would have done. Like you, I had loads of therapy. I just about got myself together – went to Uni – got massive student loans - got a job as a waitress to pay my way. And here I am."

"You also pulled off a great job – and then got kicked out because you wouldn't sleep with your boss."

"That sums up my life."

"OK. Really hard not to say anything. Shit!"

The mutual, ensuing silence was punctuated with a final swig of whisky which was enough to complete their unspoken, empathetic sentences.

"Well, Annie. Suddenly our safety zone looks very safe indeed. Turns out we are both emotional retards incapable of either physical or emotional involvement."

Anaya threw her head back to dissipate her tension and allowed a laugh to share her relief that the shared confessions were over.

"I guess so. I don't know why I laughed. It's not funny."

"No. It's definitely not funny. Life has dealt us some shit, but at least we are still here."

Anaya ruminated and stared out of the window at the lights of London.

"That party didn't exactly turn out the way I thought it would, but now I'm glad I went. I think I've made a friend."

"Me too. It feels very odd. Look, its late. Shall we turn in and at least try to get some sleep? We can talk about Cornwall and everything tomorrow."

"Yes. I'm exhausted."

"Me too. Anything you need just help yourself. Otherwise, I'll see you in the morning."

Both Dorus and Anaya said their good nights politely, made their way to their bedrooms and sank into uneasy but willing sleeps aided by emotional exhaustion and Arbelour.

*****

Despite the lateness that sleep had visited Dorus, he rose soon after seven o'clock and, after preparing a cup of tea, sat pensively analysing the Sunday morning joggers, dog walkers and delivery vehicles that shifted like a legion of ants on the wetted streets below the penthouse of Faulty Towers. Time drifted slowly as the surreal vision unfolded far below his elevated observation platform. Anaya appeared soon after Dorus and wandered across the open-plan living space, which now hung heavily with air subdued by the previous night's revelations, to join him on the sofa.

Dorus spoke almost ethereally in a half whisper. "Morning, Annie. Sorry, did I disturb you?"

Anaya allowed a sleep laden, pensive pause before offering her reply. "No, not at all. In fact, I slept really well after my mind stopped rushing around. I just woke at my normal time. Can I get myself a cup of tea?"

"Sure. Of course. Can you get me another too? Tea bags are in the pot by the kettle. Milk, no sugar please."

"Sure."

Anaya took Dorus' mug and silence dominated the air again peppered by the hiss and crackle of water making its way to boiling point. Anaya prepared two mugs of tea stirring each slowly and methodically as though concocting a potion, re-joined Dorus and handed him his mug as if resolving a troubling situation. Her thoughts began floating into the space between them.

"I was thinking about the Cornwall project before I went to sleep."

"I hope you are going to tell me you'll have a go at it."

"Well - and don't laugh - you know I told you I have never been to Cornwall."

"Yes."

"Promise not to laugh."

"I promise."

"Well, I've never actually been anywhere. I've never been on holiday anywhere."

"What? You must have."

Anaya spoke thoughtfully as though apologising for past misdemeanours. "No. I was born in the Whittington Hospital here in London and brought up in Islington and for one month every year my parents would take me to Lahore to do family visits. I never thought of that as a holiday – it was more of a duty. I called it the *Lahore Chore*. I was just lugged around and paraded in front of relations I didn't really know. I was their performing pet dog, I think. Then, after they went back there and left me, I was either waitressing to make ends meet or studying. No time and no money to go galivanting off. And that's it. Pretty sad, eh?"

"Well, I'm not *inviting* you to Cornwall now. I'm *telling* you to come. You deserve a holiday."

Ignoring Dorus' command, Anaya continued her reflective discourse.

"Then I was thinking about the job I had. I was so pleased and proud when I got it, but then all I did every day was number crunch whilst the partners did all the creative stuff. Really boring. So, the Cornish project suddenly looks really exciting. But I'm not sure I can do it. I've never done anything like that before. So, I guess what I'm saying is that I really fancy having a look at it, but I'm not confident I can do it."

"There's only one way to find out - try. Anyway, you'd be doing me a favour. I don't normally invite people down there, but I'd love to have you to come and stay. I mean it. But if you don't want to do it after you've had a look around, that's fine. If you go ahead, then I'll pay you for your work."

"I'm actually very tempted. It's not as though I've got any other work offers at the moment. Sorry, I don't mean it like that. I mean it really does sound tempting."

"Great."

Dorus spoke purposefully as though a contract had just been signed disallowing Anaya any space to offer a refusal.

He returned to watching the human ants until Anaya broke into his thoughts.

"Why do you hate this place so much? It's incredible."

"Oh, it's just soulless. It's a place to meet clients. It's immoral."

"Immoral? How do you figure that?"

"Well, see out there?" Dorus gestured across London with a sweep of his hand. "There's maybe ten thousand people sleeping rough out there in London and this place sits here all high and mighty – all full of itself – empty for maybe eleven months of the year. It sits here day after day waiting for the rich and famous to come and take it for granted. It's just not right."

"No, I suppose not. But what's the answer? You can hardly house all the homeless up here."

Dorus ignored the question as if assuming it was rhetorical.

"Actually, I did start a charity once. It was aimed at providing education and health care in developing countries. Didn't last long. I lost loads of money."

"How come? What happened?"

Dorus swung round and his voice suddenly broke from its introspection and squared itself up to convey the gravity of what he was about to impart.

"I'll fill you in later - Annie, there's something I want to tell you. I need to tell you before you commit to coming to Cornwall. I have to."

"Jesus! That sounds serious. At least I'm totally awake now!"

"Sorry, but I guess there's no really good time. It's good stuff though, so don't worry. I didn't mean to rattle you."

"OK. Hit me with it."

"Right. Settle down. It's a short story but it's important." Dorus paused and engaged Anaya's eyes as a sign that something of significance was about to unfold. "You know the Good Samaritan in the Bible?"

"Of course. This guy was beaten up and robbed. Then a priest sees him and walks by just like others did until finally a Samaritan came and helped him. Right?"

"Exactly. But there is a parallel account of it which goes a bit further. The Good Samaritan helped the guy because he had fallen on hard times and had been left for dead. The poor guy didn't deserve it. He had ended up half dead in the street, but it had been of no fault of his own. The Samaritan housed him and gave him food and then, over several months, allowed the guy to have space in his life and in his head to get himself together and find a way to rebuild his life. Rebuild it in a way he really wanted to. Then, when he had got his life together, he turned around to the Samaritan and asked how much he owed him now he was in a position to pay him back. The Samaritan refused to take any money and instead told the guy to do the same for someone else when the opportunity arose."

"Nice story, but I can't see where all this is going. I hadn't put you down as a religious type."

"No, this is not about religion. And no, I'm not religious. You've heard of paying a debt back? Well, this is about paying a debt forward. The guy did pay the debt forward after a few years. Then it happened again and again. The debt has been passing forward for centuries. Honestly. I'm not making this up. I'm not retelling a parable – this is for real. It's still happening now."

"OK." There was increasing curiosity and caution in Anaya's voice.

"So, when I hit rock bottom and both my life and I had fallen apart, I met this woman who took me under her wing. She was carrying the debt and she passed it to me."

"What do you mean?"

"She kind of adopted me. She gave me a place to stay and food to eat. All I had to do was get myself together. Which I did - eventually. She told me the Samaritan story and explained she was the one currently carrying the debt. She passed the debt to me. I've been carrying the debt ever since. Actually, we don't call it a debt. In reality, it is a big responsibility. We call it a *burden*. She offloaded the *burden* onto me and now I'm carrying it. I'm now the Burden Giver." Dorus emphasised the last two words performatively to ensure Anaya would absorb their meaning.

"Wow. That's some story."

 "Now, here I am, sitting here, looking at you. Your life hasn't exactly gone according to plan. None of it was your fault. You've done everything right but you've kind of hit the buffers. So, I'm thinking, are you the one for me to pass the burden on to?"

"Holy crap, Dorus! I've not even got dressed yet and you dump that on me!"

"I know, believe me. I was there once. It took me weeks to get my head around it before I agreed that she could pass the burden to me. But once I got there, I never looked back. Now I am the Burden Giver. Might you be the one I've been looking for to pass the burden on to?"

"I'm speechless. I met you less than twelve hours ago at a party. I let you persuade me to come back to your place – that was amazing enough. Then you invite me to come and stay with you in Cornwall – and now this!"

"Yes. Sorry. I probably didn't handle that very well. I told you I'm not used to talking to people. But I couldn't let you come to Cornwall without you knowing what was in my mind. It would have been dishonest. At least now you know so you can choose to walk away. Waiting until you got to Cornwall before I said anything might have been a bit of an ambush.

I've often thought about how I might tell someone about the possibility of passing the burden on to them – it was never like this. I'm totally clumsy when it comes to talking to people."

"I seriously don't know what to make of what you just told me. Well, at least I'm totally awake now. Can I get another cup of tea?"

"Genuinely. I do know how you feel. Tea? Yes, of course. Here, give me your cup. I'll get them."

Their conversation met a temporary hiatus but the air in the penthouse now screamed and raced with scrambled thoughts.

Dorus returned, stood in front of her, bowed deferentially and handed her the mug of tea as though it were a peace offering before resuming his seat and resuming the conversation.

"Trouble is, I'm leaving in a couple of days. I'm heading to Provence to chop wood so I'm not sure where we go with it now. Look, here's a thought. The only person I have ever confided in is Ruth. She knows all about the burden giving thing. Why don't you give her a call? She'll talk sense. She always does. As a human rights lawyer she seems to have a very clear view of just about everything. Perhaps not call her right now, she's probably got the mother of all hangovers. Maybe later today."

"OK. I think I've got about a million questions, but I don't know what any of them are yet."

"That sounds about right. I have one question for you, though. It's a fairly simple one. I don't have much in for breakfast but will coffee and croissants do?"

"I guess so. I'm not even sure about that at the moment. I don't think I even know my name anymore. Sorry, now I'm being rude. I mean, yes, coffee and croissants would be great, thanks."

"Don't worry. I remember feeling like that. Sorry to land this on you so early in the morning. But of course, you can just tell me to sod off. I wouldn't blame you."

"Enough! Yes, to coffee and croissants. That's as far as I can think."

"Great. I'll pop them in the oven. If you want to get yourself up, we'll have breakfast upstairs. The weather is amazingly good now after all that rain."

"Upstairs?"

"Yes. The roof garden."

"The roof garden? You mean this place has one whole floor for bedrooms, another for living *and* a roof garden?"

"Yes. I'm sure I told you last night."

"I don't remember. In fact, my head is so scrambled right now I don't think I know anything."

"Sorry again. Maybe a croissant will help. Breakfast will be served in the roof garden in about thirty minutes. OK?"

"OK. Just promise me there are no more bombshells to hit me with."

"I promise. That's it. And don't worry. Like I say. You can have breakfast and then simply walk away and forget the nightmare called Dorus."

Anaya returned to her bedroom to shower and dress. Standing under the hot, rainforest shower allowing the water to drain down over her body gave Anaya pause in the unfolding uncertainty that had engulfed her otherwise predictable but shattered life. Dorus returned to the kitchen to bake croissants and to contemplate his social clumsiness and to ruminate on the trajectory he might have impulsively triggered in his otherwise predictable but reformed life.

On the roof Dorus laid out a table with freshly ground coffee, croissants, jam and orange juice. The morning air was crisp and cleansed by the previous night's rain and the sun warmed the breakfast venue as a fully dressed, wet haired Anaya appeared and joined him.

"I feel a bit better now." Then after pausing to take in the scene, she exalted. "Wow! This is amazing. Breakfast in a roof garden overlooking the Thames. I just don't believe this is happening. This is a million miles away from my poxy box-room in Islington."

"I'm glad you are feeling a bit better now. Sorry again."

"You are really going to have to stop apologising."

"I'll try, but I mean it."

Anaya was unable to stop herself immediately segueing to the burden giving theme that now preoccupied her.

"I didn't ring Ruth, but I sent her a text thanking her for the party and asking if we could talk later today. She actually phoned straight back. Apparently, she never even went to bed. She sounded sober too – well, as much as she ever does. She speaks so fast!"

"That's our Ruth. I don't remember the last time she actually breathed."

"So anyway, I started telling her what you said about the burden thing and she just took over. She said that accepting the debt – sorry, the *burden* – was a chance in a lifetime and I'd be mad not to think about it. She said I deserved it after all I've been through."

Dorus sipped his coffee and held his countenance.

"Trouble is, that's made it worse. If she'd told me it was all a load of bull, life would be simple. I'd just leave here and carry on looking for a job. But she seems to think I should take it seriously. I think it has left me with even more than a million questions now and I still can't quite think of a single one."

"I know. I really do. Look, I have an idea."

"Should I be worried? What now?"

"Well, you are obviously going back to Islington soon. Why not let it all settle in your head and then, when you are ready, we'll meet up and you can interrogate me. Just remember that I'm off in a couple of days. I mean, if you can, let's meet up later today and see if we can talk some sense about it. Or, if you prefer, you can just tell me you aren't interested. I'd understand, believe me."

"OK. Give me your number. I'll call you later."

Numbers were exchanged, breakfast was consumed, farewells were given and Anaya left with swirling thoughts distracting her from her journey back to her attic room in the shared house in Islington.

Later that afternoon Anaya called Dorus' mobile phone as he walked lazily alongside the Thames dodging the joggers and cyclists. His thoughts had drifted to the excitement he felt at maybe finally being relieved of his burden but his stomach was in knots as he allowed himself to explore the potential implications.

"Dorus? It's me."

"Hi. How are you feeling now?"

"I'm good. Ruth phoned me again. She really is very insistent. Can we meet up again later? I don't know what to make of it all yet, but she says I've got to talk it over with you otherwise she'll disown me. A tad insensitive of her after my parents actually did disown me, but hey, it's Ruth, so I forgive her."

"She's very persuasive, isn't she? Yes, of course. I'll pick up some fish and make us something to eat if that's OK. Do you want to come to Faulty Towers, say about six?"

"Perfect. See you then."

The conversation ended abruptly with no other farewells as though some important business had been concluded and they each resumed their respective days which were now linked by an invisible leash.

*****

Dorus went in pursuit of fish from the local Waitrose store but, mindful that Anaya might not show up that evening, he decided to cook a simple dish consisting of monkfish in a Thai coconut sauce served on a bed of fettuccine. If she decided to come it would take him only about thirty minutes to prepare but if she didn't, then he could freeze the fish and thereby mitigate any waste.

Anaya, now in the chicest part of Islington and alone with her thoughts in her very un-chic attic room, tried to untangle the conflicts that were swirling around in her head and which had temporarily signposted the crossroads her life had reached. The actors running around her were suffocating and threatening to the point of triggering panic. She heard herself speaking out loud to herself in calming tones as she began the process of composing herself and trying to locate some rational thoughts. Conscious thought took control of the autonomic processes controlling her breathing as she grasped at images of calmness and tranquillity to hold back the tide of confusion and discomfort enveloping her.

Her confusion voiced its thoughts out aloud in the privacy of her claustrophobic boxroom.

"That was the craziest twelve hours of my life. I just went to a party and now everything is turned inside out, upside down and back to front. Twelve hours ago, I knew where I was going – albeit I was heading for a brick wall. Now some random guy is telling me to jump out of a plane without a parachute and hope for the best. But Ruth says it is kosher. Ruth says *he* is kosher. Well, I'll give him the benefit of the doubt and see him this evening, but I can always just walk away and resume normal service. Not that normal service is actually that normal at the moment. In fact, its bloody shite. My life is going precisely nowhere. Has my life really got so crap that I am pinning my hopes on some bloke I met at a party?"

Anaya collected a towel and her bathing costume and set off to the local swimming pool to find distraction from the lifechanging decision she was now faced with. The repetitive action of front crawl and the mounting number of lengths gave a temporary hiatus to the turmoil numbing her mind.

*****

As evening approached, a confused and nervous but surprisingly excited Anaya pressed the intercom in the street at the entrance to Faulty Towers.

"You came!"

"Of course. I said I would. Didn't you think I'd come?"

"I couldn't have blamed you for just getting on with your life and dismissing me as some sort of freak."

"Well, it was tempting. Let's just call it the *Ruth effect,* shall we? Ruth must be obeyed!"

"Yup. Ruth calls the shots." Dorus paused to consider what was to come before recommencing. "Tell you what – and this is just a suggestion – why don't we stop talking on the intercom and why don't you just come on up?"

"Sounds like a plan. In your own time Dorus."

Dorus pressed the entry button, the elevator reflexly descended to greet her and the doors opened to beckon her into the gilded box which would transport her to an uncertain future. Stepping into the enclosed space of the penthouse elevator felt claustrophobic as she realised she was totally alone. She was alone in a tiny, moving box. She was alone in life. She felt she needed rescuing. As it climbed, Anaya felt her lungs grip her heart but the swiftness of the ascent interrupted her increasing impulse to turn and run.

Dorus stood at the exit to the elevator and the entrance to the penthouse like a gatekeeper to another world. Anaya stepped out and Dorus made a clumsy attempt at a fashionable cheek kiss but instead landed a kiss on her ear.

"Hi. Sorry about the cheek kiss thing. I've never actually got the hang of it. I never know if it is one cheek or both. I actually misread a third cheek kiss once and headbutted a famous pop star."

"Wow, Dorus, that is some story to greet me with."

"Sorry. I'm feeling nervous for some reason."

"Glad I'm not the only one. Are you actually going to let me in?"

"That's a very good idea, Annie. Do come in."

Dorus stepped aside and gestured with a sweep of his hand that she should cross the threshold into his world.

Once in the penthouse they traversed the space in silence, resumed their now familiar seating positions and Dorus began a sentence which he then immediately abandoned.

"Well?"

"Well indeed, Dorus. I have to confess I am probably even more cynical now than I was when I left this morning but Ruth said I should at least talk about this debt, sorry, *burden* thingy. So here I am."

"I'm glad you are here. Straight down to business too. How about a drink before we get started? Glass of wine?"

"Please. Thanks."

White wine was collected from the fridge, poured into high stemmed wine glasses which were raised and clinked with the deliberate avoidance of eye contact before Dorus resumed.

"So, of the million questions you have, have you managed to get at least one straight enough in your head to ask me?"

"To be blunt, no. But maybe I have one question which might help. It's just this. You say you were helped by a Good Samaritan."

"By a Burden Giver. Yes."

"Exactly. By a Burden Giver. So, what happened? How did it work?"

"Fair question. I'll answer it honestly. But first let's just enjoy the wine for a moment. Sorry, but I don't know why I'm feeling nervous. Maybe I have carried the burden for so long now I'm not sure what to do with it."

"Well, I think I probably trump you on the nervous stakes. This is all a bit freaky."

"I know. Drink up. This is a nice white. We've got monk fish for dinner but it's in a spicy sauce so we could switch to red then if you want."

Dorus rose to fetch the wine bottle to refresh their glasses whilst Anaya continued.

"So, Dorus. You lied to me."

Dorus swung around surprised and offended.

"When we met in the summer house at the party you said you were boring. Well, in less than a day I've learned you are a rich widower, a ghost writer for famous pop stars, you have a mystery house in Cornwall, another house in France, you are some sort of Burden Giver dude and now I learn you can cook. Not so boring really."

Not knowing how to respond to Anaya's excellent ice-breaker, Dorus poured the wine performatively into the wine glasses as though he was imparting wisdom and resumed his seat.

"OK. Here we go. I'll tell you the story." After briefly raising his eyes to the ceiling to straighten his thoughts into some sort of coherent order, he drew a deep breath to steady himself and resumed. "As you know, my life fell apart and I went into meltdown. Serious meltdown. I was medicated and passed from psych to psych to try to help me. I lost my job and I was about to lose my flat. That's when I met the Burden Giver. Completely by chance."

"And can you tell me who it was?"

"No, sorry. It's just part of the deal. We have to protect each other's identities. It's only right. Anyway. She told me all about the Burden Giver thing and it blew what was left of my little mind."

"I can identify with that."

"But I was desperate. It took me a couple of weeks to come to terms with the idea that a complete stranger would house and feed me and want nothing in return. But I slowly got there. Given that I didn't have a plan B then I eventually went along with it. She rented me a flat, paid all the bills and provided food and clothing for me. I was totally pampered."

They both gulped a large mouthful to hide their reciprocated awkwardness and Dorus continued.

"Every case is different, but in my case, I continued with all sorts of therapies to try to sort myself out. One of them was music therapy. I started expressing my hurt, my hate, my anger and so on by writing songs. Ruth's husband, Derek, as you know, is a musician."

"Well, a wannabe musician-cum-freeloader if you ask me. If Ruth wasn't a highly paid human rights lawyer, he'd be couch surfing with the rest of his mates."

"Yes, I agree, but I have to be grateful to him though. He does have connections in the music industry and so he sent a few of my songs out to various people. Totally amazingly, some got bought. Next thing I know, I'm flavour of the month and I can hardly write songs fast enough to supply the demand. I think I have a bottomless cesspit of angst and misery to draw on. My misery sells well apparently. The rest is history. I went from strength to strength, pulled myself up and here I am."

"That's nuts!"

"Total nuts. Of course, the music industry is very fickle so I know I'll be dropped just as quickly as I was picked up but at least I'm secure enough now to find yet another direction to travel in if I have to."

"OK. Another question. How long was it before your Burden Giver let you fly solo?"

"In my case, it was more-or-less a year to the day. But there are no rules. It could be much less – it could be much longer."

"Right. I'm on a roll now. Another question. How much did it cost her to be your sugar daddy?"

"Oi! Don't be cheeky. Not a sugar daddy. There are no strings attached. She asked for nothing at all in return."

"Yes, sorry. Didn't mean to be cheeky. I was just trying to lighten the mood."

"It's a fair question. She never told me and I didn't ask. But I guesstimate it to be about forty grand in total. Probably more, but I wasn't keeping count."

"So, she stumped up forty grand plus with no strings attached?"

"Well, not quite. There is one very big string attached. In fact, it is a rope. In fact, it is a very heavy coil of rope. Once you accept the burden then you have to carry it around with you until you find someone else you think might deserve to take it from you."

"OK. I get it. I guess I am just struggling to trust you. No offence."

"You'd be mad to trust me frankly. But just maybe a little madness is what you need right now."

"Not a great answer, if I may say so."

"Agreed."

"So, you are basically saying I should trust you and just jump off a cliff and see where I land."

"Exactly."

"That's reassuring."

"I know. The thing is, you need the courage to jump and to trust in me to support you until you decide when and where you want to land."

"OK. Last question - for now - why am I so excited about doing something so utterly reckless and stupid then?"

"I have no answer for that. Other than perhaps, you will be in control of everything. I basically just let you get on with it. Tell you what. Why don't you come and sit up at the kitchen counter whilst I put dinner together?"

"Now that is a decision I can make. Shall I bring the wine over with me."

"Excellent plan."

Having relocated and Anaya having refreshed their wine glasses, Dorus began cooking and continued the conversation.

"You know I said there were no more bomb shells?"

"Oh, God. What now, Dorus?"

"Well, I was thinking. You know I said I was off to my house in Provence in a couple of days?"

"Yes."

"Well why not come?"

"Christ, Dorus! Have I got this right? I meet you at a party, I come back to your place, you offer me unlimited resources to take a year out from reality and then ask me to run away with you to France?"

"When you put it like that it does sound a bit nutty. Well, all I was thinking was that if you came along for the road trip, we could talk about the burden giving thing as much as you like. Then, when we get to Cornwall you can take a look at the architectural job too. By then you should have decided to accept the burden or not. If you accept it, we can get on with it but if not, you can just come back to London and keep job hunting. You'd actually be doing me a favour. It would be great to have a travel buddy for once and if you can sort my Cornish house out too that would be amazing."

"You have the habit of saying utterly crazy things in a way which makes me want to go along with it."

"Sorry about that."

With food bubbling on the induction range behind him, Dorus rested on a stool opposite Anaya and looked her in the eyes.

"I have a question for you."

"OK. Sounds serious. Fire away. Just don't expect any sensible answer."

"Is there a web site that architecture jobs get advertised on?"

"Yes."

"And is there an app which you have on your phone?"

"Yes."

"And have you set a notification in the app to tell you when a job that fits your profile comes up?"

"Yes."

"And do you still check the app every five minutes just in case?"

Anaya at last felt relaxed enough to release a genuine laugh.

"Yes! I've actually become a bit OCD about it. So where are you going with this?"

"Well, if you came on the road trip you could still be job hunting and, if one came up and you were still unsure about the burden thing, then you could bail at any point and come back to London - so not so scary, then."

"You've really thought this through, haven't you?"

"Not really. I'm making this up as I go along."

"I can't really think of any negatives at the moment other than the fact it is totally insane. Except that I can't really afford to take a holiday."

"But it won't cost you anything. I'd pay for everything as we went along. If you decide to take the burden, then whatever I pay just becomes part of the burden you'll carry. If you decide not to take the burden then I'll pay you for the architectural consultation and deduct your expenses. It's a win-win as far as I'm concerned. Either way it won't cost you a penny and you'll owe me nothing."

"Oh, Christ. I really wish I could find a good reason to say no."

"Believe me. I genuinely know how you feel. Let's eat."

Dorus brought over a bottle of red wine, two new glasses and, after some culinary gymnastics, served two bowls of monkfish, Thai coconut sauce and pasta.

He broke Anaya's confusion with a new tack.

"Let's talk about what the road trip might look like."

"A holiday. I really could do with some time out. Life's been a bit of a bitch if I'm honest with myself."

"Right. It'll work like this. We head off to the Eurotunnel and then drive down to a hotel on the east of Paris for the night just to break the journey. Two rooms, obviously."

"Oh, wow, I've always wanted to go to Paris."

"Well, I didn't mean actually go to Paris, but we could if you want. There's a hotel I use sometimes. We could book a couple of rooms there for a few days. It's on a Metro line so it's easy to get into Paris."

"Sounds amazing."

"OK. A few days in Paris then doing the sites. Maybe you could give me a lesson in architecture too. I'm genuinely interested. I'm fascinated how architecture and music work together to influence society."

"Happy to."

"Then we motor on down to Provence. It's a bit of a hike. How would you feel about sharing the driving?"

"I'd be happy to – except for one small detail – I can't drive. Born and bred in London, remember. There was never any need."

"Can't drive? OK, well maybe put 'learn to drive' on your to-do list when we reach Cornwall. No problem. We'll head on down to Provence and hang out there for a few days and I'll chop wood to feed *la bête*."

"*La bête*?"

"*The beast*. It's a massive cast iron range. The house is very off-grid. There's a small windmill, a bit of solar and water from a spring. But heating, cooking and hot water all come from *la bête* - she needs constant feeding - with wood - hence the chopping. Plus, chopping wood is very cathartic. Not that I'm suggesting you need to chop wood."

"Sounds like another world."

"It is. It's like the world stands still. Like I say, I think of it as my spiritual home. I go there two or three times a year to top up my soul."

"Seriously, Dorus. It sounds wonderful."

"Right. Then we head on right across France to Roscoff to catch the ferry to Plymouth and then head on down to *chez moi* in Cornwall. From Provence to Roscoff is a two-day trip so we'll break the journey overnight somewhere. Come to think of it, we could divert a bit and visit Versailles and Giverny if you want."

"Versailles! The Palace of Versailles is definitely on my bucket list. It's one of those architectural *must-see* places. Giverny?"

"Giverny is where Monet's garden is. Perfectly preserved. Complete with his house just as it was when he lived there. You can wander through the actual garden he spent his life painting."

"Wow! And we can go there? It's on our route?"

"Yes. It's just a very small diversion. So, we could book a couple of rooms there and spend a day at Versailles and a day at Giverny before heading up to the ferry at Roscoff. Then on to my place where I'll put you to work to perform some architectural magic. Also, hopefully by then you will have accepted the burden. But if you decide it's not for you, then you head back to London."

"The whole trip sounds absolutely amazing, Dorus."

"It is. I love it. But it would be even better with some company. So, if you came, you'd be doing me a favour. Are you thinking you might do it?"

"I'm more tempted than I should be. How long do I have to decide?"

"Where are we? It's Saturday now. So, I'll probably aim to head off on Wednesday. But don't take too long thinking about it because I'll need to book the Eurostar and the hotel at Paris. The rest can wait."

"Book it!"

"Really?"

"Well, let me recap again. I lose my job, go to a party, meet a complete stranger, go back to his penthouse, he ends up saying he'll pay for me to take a year off out of life and then I agree to go on holiday with him. Not at all unusual, Dorus."

"Well, when you put it like that; but on the plus side, Ruth does say it's a good idea."

"Either I have lost all contact with my senses or this is the most life-transforming opportunity of my life. I'll go with the latter. Yes. Book it. If I stop to think I'd probably have to section myself. So just book it."

"OK. You're on."

Having finished their meal, Dorus fetched his laptop and within minutes a Eurostar crossing was booked for Wednesday morning and hotel rooms on the east side of Paris reserved.

Their immediate future was sealed and a road trip planned which would begin a journey that would transform their lives.

Still swirling with confusion, Anaya left to head back to Islington having arranged to return to Faulty Towers on Tuesday night in order to sleep ready for an early morning departure on Wednesday.

the road trip

Dorus reminded himself of the fact that Ruth had asked to see him before he headed off to France and she was not someone he would ever want to ignore or disrespect. She had been a great emotional buttress to him over the years and he always felt that he had been a poor bedfellow in terms of reciprocity. Ruth was somewhat redoubtable and Dorus was equivalently submissive which made dialogue between them significantly partisan, but Dorus would make the effort to meet with her before his departure as she had demanded. Considering that Anaya was due to arrive on Tuesday evening, Dorus messaged Ruth to suggest she might come to Faulty Towers for late afternoon tea that same day. That way, he calculated, Anaya might also be present and could help bear the load of the conversation with Ruth. He simultaneously messaged Anaya to inform her of his plan.

A return message from Ruth confirmed she would arrive at Faulty Towers at about five o'clock after she had finished at her Chambers and a second message from Anaya similarly confirmed she would arrive early in the evening in order to meet with Ruth.

Dorus smiled a 'mission accomplished' smile to himself before heading out to drift around the opulence of St Katharine Docks and then to join the crowds milling along the banks of the River Thames in order for him to find social opacity. The marina housed several overly extravagant motor yachts and was lined with upmarket restaurants and stores each beckoning tourists and the nouveau riche to depart with their money. Dorus would, as always, forget that he wasn't invisible as he inspected the couples lovingly sharing drinks and plates of decorative cuisine. Mostly, they were sufficiently absorbed with their companions not to notice him, but occasionally complaining stares would meet his prying eyes and he would hurry past to seek greater anonymity away from the dockland microcosm.

He eventually returned to Katharine Heights and, as Tuesday afternoon began to begrudgingly give way to evening, Dorus steeled himself for the energy Ruth would suddenly project into the tranquillity of the lofty seclusion of the Faulty Towers penthouse. The imminent arrival of Anaya similarly brought feelings of foreboding. He had invited Anaya into the privacy of his life that he so protected. He was about to begin a simple and familiar road trip but a complex and unfamiliar journey with her and he doubted he had the sentient capacity to cope.

Feelings of inevitability bore down on Dorus as the repetitive buzzing of the intercom signalled the arrival of either Ruth or Anaya. He guessed it was the former as the relentless, bludgeoning buzzing made a gallant effort to break his resolve to be calm. Without offering any discourse over the voice or video link to the ground floor, he pressed the entry button and stood in front of the mirror by the elevator door rehearsing what he hoped would be a warm smile and a convincingly relaxed body posture.

The walnut doors hissed and Ruth propelled herself into the penthouse embracing and kissing Dorus on the cheek in what appeared to be one seamless movement. As Dorus picked up his *amour propre,* Anaya emerged in Ruth's wake as an apparition rising from a dream.

"Hi. Ruth and I met up earlier. She had some time off from her Chambers so she offered to pick me up and drive me over here with my luggage – in her Porsche – hence the small bags. How are you?"

Dorus, unable to find any voice to offer a response, lifted in the two bags of Anaya's belongings and then began to find himself relieved that Anaya and Ruth might already have concluded their discussion about the road trip and burden giving. He found a small fissure in the wall of angst he was carrying in order to cede to some level of relaxation and composure.

Still cautious of each other, Dorus and Anaya exchanged polite smiles but avoided the more intimate hugs and cheek kisses that Ruth had demonstrated with relenting exuberance. Both Dorus and Anaya silently shared a cautious excitement about what their immediate futures might present to them but this was laced with a reluctance to allow their newly formed friendship to intrude into their much-coveted privacies.

Ruth had already begun a one woman show whilst taking in the panoramic view of London.

"Come here you two. Just look at this. Tell me Anaya, what do you see? I bet you see an amazing city full of inspiring buildings and opportunities. And you, Dorus? I bet you see a dystopian nightmare trying to crush your spirit. Well, you are both right and both wrong."

Dorus and Anaya tried to interject but failed. Had their views been shared, Ruth would have been comforted by the accuracy of the analysis of her two companions.

"Look, you two. Let me guess. You are both feeling a bit terrified. Don't. End of. Just don't. Now, I've got some bad news. I can't stay. Big case coming up. We have a stratagem meeting this evening and I've got to go and prep. Should be prepping now, but I wasn't going to let you two head off on your adventure without seeing you first. Looks like I'm heading off to Tehran too. So, I must shoot. Lovely to see you. Come here Dorus – stop looking so confused. Anaya is lovely. You'll have a great trip. And you, Anaya – Dorus is a darling – he'll take care of you and believe me, it'll be worth it. Both of you just ride life like a roller-coaster and let it thrill you. You have both earned some happiness, so grab it and stop analysing it!"

Neither Dorus nor Anaya liked roller-coasters but liked disagreeing with Ruth even less.

Ruth embraced and kissed both Dorus and Anaya separately and then hugged them simultaneously before departing as dramatically as she had arrived leaving Dorus and Anaya feeling somewhat dizzied.

Dorus caught his breath enough to find some hesitant words.

"Did you get all that?"

"Just about. I think I am lovely; you are a darling and we have to go on a roller-coaster together."

"Yup, I think that was it."

Dorus diverted his rising apprehension which had been induced by finally being alone with Anaya by moving to the kitchen and filling the kettle contemplatively wondering what words he could find to begin a conversation. He finally landed on a single word and Anaya found a singular response.

"Tea?"

"Please."

The exchange, although diminutive in its importance was sufficient to permit Dorus to offer further discourse.

"I don't have a plan for this evening. We could get some food in to cook or maybe a takeaway? Or, there is that new Punjabi restaurant just around the corner if you fancy grabbing something to eat there. What do you think?"

Considering that she might already have intruded too much into Dorus' penthouse privacy over the last few days and perhaps Dorus might be resenting the fact, she opted for a restaurant meal. Neutral ground might offer some sense of safety from the confusion of their immediate future. The positive tone in her voice masked the insecurity in her mind.

"Let's go out. That sounds fun. My treat."

"Great. I'll see if they have a table. But no – I'm paying remember. The journey starts here. I'm paying and we'll either settle up out of the fee for your architectural consultation in Cornwall or it just becomes part of the burden you'll take on."

"Just tonight. I'd love to treat you. We can start the journey tomorrow."

"Well, we can talk about it over dinner, but seriously, you are going to have to get used to this. You'll find it hard. You'll want to pay your way, but sooner or later you'll have to come to terms with the fact that it doesn't work like that. As far as I'm concerned, the journey starts now."

Dorus paused and drew breath suddenly startled at how dogmatic he had sounded, but Anaya was quick to defuse the moment.

"You know, Dorus. It's not just the burden thing. I'm just not used to people being nice to me. Not that people are nasty to me – most people anyway – it's just that I keep myself to myself so people don't get the chance to be nice. I tend to have colleagues or acquaintances rather than friends. If anyone shows me kindness, I end up feeling guilty. I know it's stupid but, well, you know."

"I know exactly what you mean. I think it's easier to be nice to people than to let them be nice to me. But I mostly avoid situations where being *nice* is even an option."

The kettle blew time on their deepening exchange, the tea was brewed and then consumed creating an agreement that they should avoid further potentially problematic discourse at least for the time being. Dorus booked a table at the restaurant and they both silently agreed to relax back into the safety and comfort of their now routine seating arrangement at opposite poles of the L-shaped sofa overlooking the City of London. As they watched the miniature of London folk scurrying by from their heady perch their conversation resumed without the need for them to engage their eyes.

"I take it you and Ruth have already sorted the world out."

"Pretty much. I'm to trust you, enjoy the road trip, accept the burden but above all I'm to stop thinking. Apparently, I am my own worst enemy and I should embrace solicitude. I had to look *solicitude* up on my iPhone when Ruth went to the loo. But I think it means I need to accept other people's kindness to me."

"All good advice, I'd say. 'Stop thinking' is a tough one, though! I'm afraid I overanalyse things out of existence sometimes. No, actually, I do it all the time."

"Me too. I'm going to have to learn to let go. On so many levels I've found a comfortable way to exist but I know I have to step out into the unknown sooner or later. I might find it hard. I'll try not to bother you with it."

"No, actually, let's agree on one thing. Let's try to be honest and open with each other. About how we feel, I mean. I think that will be important. Trying to guess what the other one is thinking could lead to all sorts of misunderstandings. We are about to set off on something together so sharing will be important."

"Agreed. But, again, it will be hard. I am so used to hiding how I feel. I've learned to hide my feelings from myself as much as from other people."

"Hard for both of us, but perhaps that is all part of our safety zone. It should be a safe place for us to be honest. I seem to remember lots of shrinks saying something like that about their consultation rooms."

"Yeah, I guess so."

"I just overanalysed everything again, didn't I?"

"Yup. But it makes sense. Setting a few house rules is a good idea."

Sensing the need to abandon the increasing intensity of their conversation, Dorus offered an escape route.

"Come on, drink up. It's a beautiful evening. Why don't we take the scenic route along the Thames on our way to the restaurant? We can check out all those ridiculously expensive boats moored in St Katharine Docks on the way too."

"Perfect. Give me a sec. I'll just use your loo if I may."

They abandoned their mugs near the sink and Dorus covertly checked himself out in the full-length mirror by the elevator as he waited for Anaya to join him. They entered the elevator, descended to street level and ventured into the evening air to make their way to the restaurant where they were about to eat their last meal before embarking on a journey which felt to them to be both otherworldly and full of potential danger.

Arriving precisely on time for their seven o'clock reservation, Dorus swung open the restaurant door and half bowed to Anaya to beckon her past him into the spice laden fug. They were greeted by a young Punjabi waitress who scrutinised the reservation list in a manner that made them feel awkward as though their reservation would not be honoured. Instead, she looked up, smiled and beckoned Dorus and Anaya to follow her to their table. Once seated, two beers were ordered and they began to peruse the extensive menu.

"You know, Annie, we might try to talk about something other than the burden this evening. I fear I might just have been a bit intense about it. I mean, we can talk about it if you want but it might just be nice to get to know each other a bit before we head off into the unknown. After all, we can talk about it *ad infinitum* once we are on the road."

"Yeah sure. To be honest, I still don't know what to make of it. So, what do you want to talk about?"

"OK. You've stumped me there. I guess I didn't think that through."

Anaya's smile calmed him as she proffered an easy route to safe ground.

"No worries. I know, let's talk about the food. What do you fancy? Are we ordering our own or sharing?"

"I'm happy to share if you are. In fact, why don't you order for both of us. I can promise you there is nothing I don't eat and nothing I won't like."

The truth was that Dorus was irrationally uneasy about exposing his gustatory preferences. Even such a simple concern had become a matter of privacy to him in his semi-eremite existence.

"OK. I'll go for my favourites."

Immediately Anaya's tension gripped her, fearful that in some small way she was being tested by Dorus' request for her to select food for him.

However, she rose to the challenge offered her, and after just a few moments, she decided to order murgh makhani, chana masala, aloo gobi and a saag together with basmati rice and naan. The waitress took their order whilst another delivered a plate of papadums together with a variety of dips and then Anaya turned back to Dorus to seek approval.

"I hope that's all OK. I hope you don't mind me asking, but did you choose this restaurant because of my Punjabi background?"

"Er, no. I think you might be flattering my knowledge of geography there. I think I remember you said your parents were from Lahore. Right?"

"Yes, and Lahore is the capital of Punjab."

"Oh. Right. It might be wise for you not to underestimate my levels of ignorance. So, Lahore is the capital of Punjab and Punjab is a province in Pakistan. Right?"

"Exactly."

"No. To be honest, I hadn't made any of those connections. I chose it because it was new and just around the corner and I like Indian food. Hang on, it isn't Indian food then, is it? It's Pakistani food."

"Exactly so, Dorus. Nearly everyone just says 'Indian' even when they mean 'Pakistani'."

"Christ, I've never really thought about it. My ignorance of Pakistan and India is astonishing. Apart from reading about partitioning, I don't really know much. You were saying about how little you have travelled, but to be honest my travel has been fairly limited but both India and Pakistan are high on my list to visit. The architecture, the music, the food, the culture draws me like a moth to a flame, but I've never been."

"Well, put that on your to-do list then."

"Now you say that, I don't really have a to-do list. I think I found a life for myself and then just got stuck in it. Sometimes familiarity and routine can feel very safe. You are right. I ought to make a to-do list. I need to be more adventurous."

"Ha! I can identify with that. College-work-college-work-college-work. That's been my life for the past five years or so. I know I need to break out of the rut." She raised her eyes to the ceiling contemplatively. "Maybe losing my job is the best thing that could have happened to me."

Anaya was stopped in her stream of consciousness by Dorus smiling benignly across the table at her.

"What?"

"This is so nice, Anaya."

"What?"

"Just going to a restaurant and having someone to talk to. I was serious when I said you'd be doing me a favour coming on the road trip. You'll be good company *and* I might offload my burden onto you *and* you might redesign my house in Cornwall. Triple whammy for me."

"Actually, I'm really looking forward to it now. Still pretty terrified to be honest, but I've got to the point where I'm actually looking forward to it. I haven't got a job anymore so, at least for a bit, I'm going to spread my wings and enjoy life. It has been a long time since I've done that. Ever since …. Well, you know."

Dorus found no need to reaffirm that he understood that her traumatic past had hindered her emotional and social development. The point of empathy which they had established was binding without the need for restatement.

"Good. Me too. If I'm honest, although I've achieved a lot over the past few years, being happy is not one of them. Time for me to change too. I'm putting 'relax and be happy' on my new to-do list right now."

"But you've been so successful, Dorus."

"If by *successful* you mean I've earned tons of dosh, then yes. If you measure success in terms of happiness, then no. Sorry, intense again. I must stop that."

Food began arriving at their table and was accompanied by a rapid description of each dish which disarmed the inevitable rise in the fervour of their conversation. Gastronomy became common ground and paved the way to a temporary hiatus to their shared unease. Their reassuring smiles merged with food, beer, conversation and something which looked to casual observers to be friendship until they returned to Faulty Towers for an early night to prepare for their joint road trip and their now interlinked but separate journeys.

*****

The earliness of the hour on Wednesday morning left both Anaya and Dorus full of thoughts but short of words as they found themselves being transported along the ill prepared course they had plotted. Descending to the subterranean carpark and loading their bags into the Audi felt autonomous and almost routine despite the unique significance of the act. Emerging into the early morning daylight felt more like an emotional dawn than a meteorological one and the urgent morning traffic presented little impediment to their progress on their exit route from London. Then, as they proceeded, the aggressive petrochemical bustle of the M20 kept their attention from what lay at the other side of the English Channel.

After arriving at Folkstone earlier than was necessary and with nervous sickness in their stomachs, paperwork was checked and a short but tiresome wait was endured before they were ushered towards *Le Shuttle* which finally broke the hiatus in their communion.

"Well, Dorus. No turning back now."

"Nervous?"

"Yes, but more tired than nervous, I think. After a good night's sleep, I'll let myself be nervous. You?"

"Yes, me too. But I don't know what there is to be nervous about."

"Oh. Just the unknown. Just jumping off a cliff. Just abandoning my life and running off with a stranger. That's all."

"Fair comment. But you are wrong about *no turning back.* That is, and always will be, your choice."

"I know. You'll be pleased to know that both my head and my heart are up for this. So, let's do it before either my head or my heart come their senses and tell me to bail before it's too late."

"Nicely put. I'm a bit apprehensive too if I'm honest. But I really don't know why."

"Well, to be fair, picking up a girl at a party and running off to France with her is a bit unusual. Especially since it is a screwed-up gal like me."

"Yeah, that just never normally happens."

Anaya and Dorus released some tension with a shared smile and restrained laughter before a Eurotunnel marshal beckoned them forwards. Soon, they found themselves cocooned and transported under the English Channel to France where disembarkation and passport checks were similarly painless but tiresome allowing their journey to proceed without further resistance.

"OK, Annie, you can't help with the driving, but you can be in charge of in-car entertainment. Do you have an iPod or music on your phone?"

"Yeah. I've got stacks on my phone."

"Right. That's a touch screen there in the middle of the dashboard so use the menu to get Bluetoothed up and choose some music. Don't take too long, I need to keep watching the Sat Nav."

With some unwarranted apprehension Anaya connected her phone to the Audi's sound system which irrationally made her feel as though she was connecting her life to his. She began scrolling through her catalogue of downloaded music, pausing and hesitating before referring back to Dorus.

"What do you fancy?

"You choose. I'll just drive. I'll be happy with anything. Nothing too pumping, though. Find something chilled."

Anaya felt her anxiety rise and apprehension monopolise her thoughts lest her music choice might not suit Dorus and might expose the first real fissure in their newly formed relationship. Anaya chose what she thought would be safe ground.

"How about Sara Swati?"

Dorus stiffened but stifled the urge to tell Anaya that Sara Swati was, in fact, his main client and that he was about to endure listening to his own compositions. However, the non-disclosure agreements he was bound by forced him to lie.

"Great. She's very good. Perfect for this rather stressful part of the drive. She's very cool if a little melancholic."

"Well, I wasn't expecting a critique of her, but if you are happy with her, then let's go with that. At least for now."

Anaya began playing the songs and allowed herself the indulgence of singing quietly along with some of the more popular tracks before adjusting the volume down to allow further conversation.

"Do you know what her name means?"

Dorus knew.

"No. Go on. Tell me."

"Well, if you put her two names Sara and Swati – pronounced *Svati* - together you get Saraswati. Saraswati is the Hindu Goddess of music. First time I came across her I thought that it was a really clever name. Now I think she's a bit arrogant to call herself after a Goddess. She has a great voice, but not good enough to think she is actually a Goddess."

"You think a pop star might be a bit arrogant, do you? Heaven forbid! It goes with the territory, I'm afraid. To stand in front of thousands of people and sing and dance for an hour and a half takes some guts, I reckon. Plus, these stars are surrounded by people telling them 24/7 how brilliant they are. They just end up believing it."

"Sounds awful."

"Yeah. It is. But to be honest, the people I work with are genuinely nice people as soon as they drop their pop star personas."

"What a strange world you live in, Dorus."

"Yup. Luckily, I'm only on the periphery of all the madness. But, as I say, only for now. When I'm no longer flavour of the month I'll be finished and I'll have to reinvent myself. To be honest, I'm struggling a bit to keep the momentum going to churn out endless rubbish."

"I noticed those leatherbound notebooks on the back seat when I got in this morning. Are they your songs?"

"Yes. I try to jot down ideas as I go along. Some of them ferment into songs and others don't. Some I really like and keep them for myself. Others I flog on as fast and for as much as I can."

"And I'm not allowed to see them. Right?"

"Yes. Sorry. Not my choice. Just the way I have to operate."

"It's not a problem. I understand. I'd really love to know which songs are yours, though. It's funny to think I might know some of your songs but I don't know which ones they are."

Both their journey and their mutual exploration of each other progressed smoothly and eventually they came to a halt outside the *Hotel de Lyon*. They pulled themselves out of the car and stretched their backs before heading to the hotel reception. Dorus broke out into fluent French despite a sign announcing that the receptionist was happy to speak English. He announced their arrival and Anaya looked startled to hear Dorus now speaking as though he had just changed his nationality.

Having checked in, found their rooms and freshened up they met up in the hotel foyer to drink coffee and to make a plan.

"OK, Dorus – so you are fluent at French too?"

"Not fluent really. When I was going through all my therapy, I signed up for one of those immersive language courses. To be so focused on something even just for a while really helped. Frankly I was signing up for anything and everything that would distract my mind. Then I came to France to practice speaking French and to get some headspace. I ended up in Provence, fell in love with a little cottage and ended up buying it. It's funny how even unrelated actions can have beneficial consequences."

"Yes, I'm beginning to learn that."

"Anyway, Annie. What do you fancy? We could just hang out here at the hotel and relax if you want. There's a swimming pool if you fancy that. Or, it's early enough to head into Paris for a quick start to being tourists."

"No contest! I'm knocking on 25 and I've never been to Paris in my life! Let's go! Er, I mean … how about going into Paris, but only if you want to, Dorus?"

"Hum. Let me think about it. OK. Let's go. I guess it had better be the Eiffel Tower to start with. Get it out of the way."

"Definitely! Would it be churlish of me to say that the Eiffel Tower is actually rather crap as a piece of architecture? It just proves that architecture doesn't have to be brilliant to get to be famous. The Eiffel Tower proves that anything can work in the right place at the right time."

"It certainly is an odd thing. Rather pointless in many ways, but going up it has to be done. Come on. Let's go."

They left the sanctuary of the hotel and navigated the Paris Metro system towards the Eiffel Tower. Anaya watched her fellow subterranean travellers wondering what it was that made them look so unmistakably Parisian. Was it their clothes? Was it their facial expressions? Was it the confident air they expressed which somehow conveyed that they were just much chicer and more stylish than her?

Eventually they surfaced into the evening air from the *Champ de Mars* station and traversed the short distance to the Eiffel Tower which immediately thrilled Anaya far more than it did Dorus.

"Oh, Dorus. It is more impressive than I thought it would be."

"There is a better view of it from the Trocadéro over there." Dorus gestured over the River Seine. "There are some pretty cool restaurants there too so maybe we could head over there in a bit and grab something to eat before heading back to the hotel."

"Yes. That sounds great. But we are going to, aren't we?"

"Going to what?"

"Go up the Eiffel Tower!"

"Obviously. Let's go right to the top. Come on, we'll need tickets. There isn't much of a queue at the moment."

Having bought their tickets, they climbed the 674 steps to the second stage, and then ascended in the elevator to the highest viewing point.

"Oh, wow. You have no idea how much this means to me, Dorus. It's like I have finally emerged from the underground pit I was in and can finally start to see."

Dorus smiled more to himself than to Anaya. Suddenly Anaya appeared to him to be like something akin to a little girl opening a Christmas present.

"Actually, you have no idea how much this means to me too. I've been up here a couple of times on my own, but to be up here with someone makes it much more of an experience. I can't really explain."

Anaya smiled more to herself than to Dorus. Pleasing her new companion made her feel good about herself. A feeling that had eluded her for many years.

"After we are done here, we can head over to the Trocadéro – you can see it well from here. Look."

Dorus gestured with a nod of his head as he formed a sentence which framed itself as a question despite being a benign decree.

"And over dinner maybe we can make a shortlist of places to visit over the next couple of days. I read there is a Monet exhibition at the Louvre so that might be a must – oh, and the Mona Lisa, of course."

"Perfect. And there are a couple of buildings I'd like to see if we have time. Is that OK? I'll tell you about them over dinner."

"More than OK."

Dorus followed Anaya around and around the viewing gallery as she inspected the same views over and over again as though they might change each time she passed them. She expressed her awe and wonder at the panoply of buildings, parks and humanity spread out beneath her. Suddenly, she broke loose from the vista and swung around to meet Dorus' approving eyes.

"OK. What's next?"

"As I say, let's head over to the Trocadéro and find a restaurant. There's no rush."

"Yes, there is! Come on. I'm not wasting a second. I want to make the most of this before I wake up and discover it is all just a dream."

Anaya grabbed Dorus' hand in the manner a young child would reach for the security of a parent, pulled him back to the elevator and then released him again without appearing to have noticed what she had done. Then, they began their descent to street level. The simple, unplanned act of holding hands for a brief moment created a pact that neither of them located in their consciousness but which pressed hard against the detachment they each carried in their subconsciousness.

Once back at ground level they headed off to cross the Pont de Bri-Hakeim over the river Seine towards the Trocadéro gardens. Half way across Anaya stopped, raised her nose high and began inhaling deeply.

"Sorry, Dorus. I just feel I am learning to breathe for the first time since ... well, you know."

Dorus did know and he understood that feeling well.

Once across the bridge they strolled, they chatted, they got to know each other in the unique way that strangers do to find commonality whilst treading neutral ground in foreign territory. Finally, they found themselves following their shared desire path along a narrow street which fell silent from the bustle of tourists and gave way to rich, piquant aromas. They found a small bistro with an appealing menu and were quickly seated at the back, away from the window, and where the dim luminescence offered some sense of faux intimacy.

One of the two young waitresses approached their table and gave them a welcoming smile and her attention along with providing menus and a long description of what, other than that written down, was on offer.

"What do you fancy then, Annie?"

"You choose. I have absolutely no idea what she just said. I'll go by what you recommend. The menu is all in French too and I did Spanish at school – and I can't remember half of that. Order something typically French."

After briefly perusing the menu and then asking questions in French, Dorus placed their order: salmon timbales followed by confit duck with redcurrant sauce. To this he added a bottle of Château Trottevieille; a singular Saint-Emilion grand cru which he knew well from his wine cellar in Cornwall. At the mention of the wine, the waitress' eyes flicked imperceptibly but just sufficiently for Dorus to notice. She directed a stare to the bar and raised her hand to her fellow waitress in a well-rehearsed, non-verbal communication. Instantly the second waitress downed the wine glass she was polishing and deferentially arrived at, and added to, the theatre unfolding alongside Dorus' and Anaya's table. The adjacent table was cleared and abutted to theirs. Their wine glasses were removed disdainfully as though they were simply inadequate and replaced by two larger ones which were vociferously polished and held to the light to prove their superior provenance. Subsequently the wine arrived, was uncorked with a flourish at the table and poured with circumspection into a decanter. Dorus' glass received a small quantity which he cradled with both hands before inhaling the bouquet through his nose. A silent, reverential nod to the waitress gave her permission to fill a wine glass for Anaya and then for him.

Anaya watched the spectacle wide-eyed and with her lips parted until the waitresses left them alone.

"What the hell just happened? We now have one table just for the wine and another just for us."

"I think we lucked-out here. We've found a restaurant which takes wine seriously so the food should be good. They always say that you must choose the food carefully to go with the wine."

"Not at all pretentious, then?" She took a sip, leaned back in her chair, savoured the moment and then spoke through the multiplex of flavours playing with her senses. "Oh, I see what you mean." She took a gulp and closed her eyes to further savour the richness and complexity of what was acting out on her palate. The second flush of the unfolding bouquet caught her by surprise and she opened her eyes and let out a gush of approval from her lungs.

The wine was excellent as was the food and their conversation captured the timbre of the evening. The direction and mood of their discourse meandered circumspectly until finally some sort of itinerary was agreed upon including a visit to the Musée du Louvre, Montmartre and the Sacré-Cœur, the Cathédrale Notre-Dame, the Avenue des Champs-Élysées, the Musée d'Orsay, the Place de la Concorde and the Arc de Triomphe. To this Anaya added some buildings of architectural merit including the Centre Georges Pompidou and the Fondation Louis Vuitton.

Their exhaustion as they travelled back to their hotel was replaced by effervescent enthusiasm as they set off the following morning to begin their whistle-stop Parisienne peregrination. Dorus impressed Anaya with a running commentary of various Paris highlights and Anaya impressed Dorus with a running commentary of hidden architectural gems. Pausing outside the Sacré-Cœur and absorbing the almost surreal vista across Paris, Anaya found herself withholding a tear behind her eyes as the reality of what was transpiring settled in her consciousness. A very mediocre lunch followed at an *al fresco* restaurant in Montmartre and they both resisted the temptation to allow an even more mediocre portrait being sketched by the myriad of artists who had set up easels every few metres.

A visit to the Musée du Louvre made claim to what was left of the enthusiasm of their feet but the Monet exhibition lifted them again before they bid farewell to the gallery after shuffling in fairy-steps with endless other tourists past the portrait of Mona Lisa. Anaya had been transported by the rows of paintings by Monet but even more so by watching Dorus' expression as he closed his eyes as he paused and stood before each one as though in deep, unshared thought.

Two further days of hectic, energy-sapping sightseeing, of eating and of conversation brought them eventually back to their hotel ready to depart on the next leg of their journey.

The gruelling eight-hour drive was to be broken with rest at an E. Leclerc hypermarket to collect provisions ready for the final, weaving ascent to the cottage which would be their shared nest for the following few days.

The tedious drive to Dorus' cottage in Provence was nuanced by Dorus and Anaya unravelling their whistle-stop tour of Paris.

"So, Annie, as a first impression what did you make of Paris?"

"Amazing. So much better than I thought it would be. I've always been told that London is the best city in the world. If nothing else, I've learned what a load of bollocks that is. There is no such thing as best, only different. I just love Paris. I can't wait to go back and spend more time there getting to know it properly. I know they always say it is a romantic city, but I wasn't actually expecting that to be true. It really does have a romantic feel to it."

"And the best bit?"

"Impossible to say. I loved every bit of it. Can I cheat? I think the best bit was just being there. Finally getting to see Paris has been long overdue."

"Yeah. I get that. For me it was being there *with* someone. It gave Paris a whole new dimension for me …. maybe that doesn't make sense."

"It totally makes sense."

"And the Mona Lisa? What did you make of her?"

"Well, a bit underwhelming really. Much smaller than I thought she'd be. She looked just like all the postcards I've seen of her. But the Monet exhibition – that just blew me away. Can we really go to his garden on the way back?"

"Giverny? Yes. It's on our to-do list along with Versailles."

Pausing their journey prior to climbing the valley side to Dorus' cottage to buy provisions for their stay in Provence was equally a pause to reflect on what was to be the next chapter of their journey, their adventure and their friendship. Deciding what items of food and drink to buy seemed like a necessary exercise to assist them in their quest to find a place of safe bonding and to explore their understanding of each other.

During the final segment of the journey their conversation flowed and the miles passed but Dorus' anxiety again began rising as they followed the winding, dusty track to the place that had been his, and solely his, for nearly five years. Allowing Anaya to enter his cottage would feel like allowing her to enter the secrecy of his soul. This was a part of his hidden self. The part that no one had ever come close to. Now, he was to welcome Anaya into that recess of his being, the secrecy of which he cherished above all else.

Somehow on their journey thus far they had avoided all mention of *Burden Giving* but Dorus knew that arriving at the cottage might summon a mutual necessity to address, either overtly or covertly, the real purpose of their journey.

the cottage in Provence

Climbing the last, steep mile along the rutted, winding track gave no hint that a building of any sort would ever come into view. The unfolding countryside blurred into a pastiche of impressionist colours and contours and then, there it was; a solitary, single storey stone building with sun-bleached terracotta roof tiles and shabby, shuttered windows. Anaya momentarily felt her heart climb her gullet and grip her throat before reassuring herself this was a benign scene and that she had been invited into it. She hoped she was being invited as a friend. Even so, some contrition bit her knowing that this spectre was deep in Dorus' private domain. Nonetheless, anamnesis of her box room in the townhouse in Islington drained from her leaving only a sense of a future memory soon to be made. Their arrival seemed to awake the cottage from its slumber after it had passively been keeping guard of the panoramic view across the expansive valley filled with rolling lavender fields and vineyards.

A wooden, open fronted barn lay to one side of the cottage and Anaya noted a large stone fireplace against the back wall almost as expansive as the barn itself. There was a smaller outbuilding hidden someway back beyond the immediate canvass and a disproportionally large, well-stocked woodstore ran parallel to one side of the house. The stacks of wood were meticulously organised and gave the impression of being carefully organised library shelves. The ground was dusty, arid and barren in contrast to the lush landscape spreading itself liberally in the valley below them. Despite its lonely neglect, everything was neat and tidy presumably as Dorus had left it after his last visit. Some dried plant material had settled in corners, but otherwise the rambling nature of the building had yielded to the neatness expected of it.

Dorus swung the Audi gently to a resting place hidden from view behind the barn and Anaya stepped out of the air-conditioned capsule into the fragrance-laced heat that enveloped her in a single, head-swirling rush. Carried by the all-pervading bouquet of lavender, she found a viewpoint in front of the house where she stood and tried to assimilate the view stretching out endlessly in front of her and which challenged her senses to come alive. Never before had she considered the world to be so large, so inviting and so giving.

"Oh, my God, Dorus. You undersold this place."

"Do you like it?"

"This is actually heaven, isn't it? This is the kind of place you come to, to die."

"Are you sure? I was a bit nervous about bringing you here."

"Why? It would be impossible not to fall in love with this place."

"Well, I plucked a full blown towny out of her natural habitat in Islington and brought her to something the polar opposite. I thought you might be a fish out of water here."

"Well. I'm a convert now. I'm officially not a towny anymore. I don't think I'll ever leave this place. Sorry, Dorus, but I might just become a squatter here."

"Great. Now, I've just got to get things going. It won't take long and then we can settle in."

"Anything I can do?"

"No. Just have a look around. Leave it to me. It's a bit of a routine. I need to get everything working. I need to wake *la bête*."

Dorus broke off and began walking towards the abeyant building. First, he skittered around the house opening shutters to let light, heat and air in and to let stale air out. Then, after flicking a few switches in a cupboard the fridge obediently began to hum and a Wi-Fi hub began blinking as it woke from its prolonged hibernation. He turned taps on to run stale water through the old pipes and then offered a match to a pre-prepared pile of kindling and paper inside the vast cast iron range. The giant range known as *la bête* began to murmur offering hope that it might supply hot water and sustenance after a period of rumination.

The cottage came alive and began its gentle, lazy welcome to its visitors.

"OK. Let's get the shopping in and then I'll take your bags to your room. Then, can I take you up there?" He gestured upwards behind the house. "There's something I want to show you before we lose the light."

"Sure. What is it?"

"It's a special place. I can't describe it; you'll have to wait to see it for yourself."

Dissatisfied but accepting of Dorus' explanation, Anaya approached the car to retrieve her personal belongings and to escort them into the cottage.

Shopping and luggage were extracted from the boot of the Audi all of which was unpacked and relocated into their new, temporary home. Dorus meticulously retrieved his leather-bound note books and chaperoned them as though they were fragile glass ornaments.

"Just a couple of things, Annie. It'll take a while for *la bête* to heat up the water, but then it should be fine for showers. We'll cook on it too - I'll get a beef bourguignon going in a minute. The Wi-Fi is on a satellite data signal so it's a bit slow. I'm afraid streaming is impossible - the code is on the hub. Er, what else …. Oh, yes …. In this little cupboard is the *bat phone*. In a real emergency just pick it up and it automatically connects to the emergency services. Let's hope we don't need that! Anything else?"

"Electricity?"

"Yes. Right. There is electricity, but there's not much of it. It's solar and a bit of wind, so use as little as possible. But there is a little generator in the shed so I never actually run out."

"Water?"

"Yes. The tap water is from a spring. It's really good, very cold and very pure, but if you prefer there is bottled water in the fridge."

"Great. Can I just have a wander around for five minutes? I'm still trying to take it all in."

"Yes, of course you can. Take your time and have a look around. *La bête* is coming up to temperature so I'll get the dinner on. You probably noticed it's freezing in the house compared to outside. It's the thick stone walls. The house will warm up now too. *La bête* is the only source of heat but it goes everywhere. Have you seen the size of her? They must have built the house around her – there is no way they could have got her in through the door."

"It's all so perfect, Dorus."

"Are you up for a stroll in about half an hour? Like I say, there is something I want to show you."

"Yes. I won't stray too far. Just give me a call when you are ready."

Dorus busied himself serving the needs of *la bête* and Anaya busied herself serving the needs of her newly liberated spirit. After not much more than half an hour Dorus slung a man-bag over his shoulder and called for Anaya. Once reunited, he led her uphill behind the house until they reached a rock outcrop. He guided her around to the back where they wriggled through a narrow crevice which yielded to a panoramic view of the expansive valley and offered what appeared to be a seat hewn out of the rock. He beckoned her to sit with him and they both finally found quiescence, momentarily mute, in awe of the panoply of stimuli that assaulted them. The view rolled over lavender fields and vineyards, the bouquet was stifling and the heat heavy and all consuming. A haze transformed the view into a rippling impressionistic painting and the lavender scent coloured the canvas with ardency. Eventually, Dorus spoke a single word which tried, but failed, to puncture the overwhelming beauty of their milieu.

"Well?"

Anaya matched Dorus' attempt at communication with a single word of her own.

"Yes."

Those two words were enough to agree that they had arrived somewhere important in their lives and that what was laid out before them transcended beauty which, at least for this moment, dispelled all feelings of the unpreparedness of the journey they had embarked upon.

An indeterminate period of time lapsed before Dorus offered Anaya the challenge he had been keen to give her.

"I call this *le trône* – the throne. I can sit here for hours. Sometimes when I sit here, I feel numb. Sometimes all my pain just drains away. I reckon there must be some ley lines crossing here or something. There just feels like some sort of supernatural power."

"You are sounding like some sort of druid, Dorus."

Dorus ignored Anaya's comment and continued as though he hadn't been interrupted.

"Anyway, it's time. You'll think this is crazy, but just go along with it. OK?"

"What?"

"Just sit here and relax. Take in the view. Then, when you are ready, close your eyes and just sit and wait. I'll be doing it too. Don't say anything. Don't do anything. Just feel."

Anaya did as requested and meaningless time again lapsed before her exclamation broke the silence forcing them both back into contemporaneity.

"Oh, for goodness' sake! That's freaky! I don't know what was meant to happen but, after a while, it was like I could still see it all – even with my eyes closed – only even clearer!"

"That's it. It blows my mind. It doesn't matter how many times I do it, it always blows my mind. It's like you become part of it."

"It's incredible. I would never have believed you if you had just told me. It's almost supernatural. I could still see the view, but the sounds and the smells were just incredible. It was like I could hear the landscape talking! It was so intense I couldn't tell where I ended and the valley started."

"I know. It never fails to amaze me. I'm glad it worked for you. I've never had anyone to stay before and I didn't know if it would work for you or not." Dorus' smile was as wide as his face. "Now, I've brought a bottle of wine to share up here. The sun sets really early because of the mountains, and the temperature goes through the floor, so we don't have long."

Dorus pulled a bottle of partially chilled white wine out of his bag together with two wine glasses. He poured carelessly and raised his glass towards Anaya. Their eyes received each other as their wine glasses kissed and Anaya's smile proposed a silent toast before the sun began its descent ultimately leaving them shrouded in dusk and a new, cleaner, cooler air.

Having exhausted the light and having bid farewell to the sun as it melted behind the distant mountains, they began to navigate the gradient back to the house. Dorus pointed out another, smaller pathway ascending to a summit.

"You might want to do that bit of the walk too. It takes about another forty-five minutes or so to get up there but it's worth it. You get a three-sixty view from the top. Maybe tomorrow whilst I'm chopping wood."

Anaya nodded in agreement and pulled her arms around her body to convince herself that doing so would protect her from the dissipating heat.

After returning to the house, Dorus lit the fire in the barn and fed it with wood cut much larger than that used to feed *la bête.* Whilst they enjoyed the increasingly fresh edge to the air as it mingled with the increasing warmth from the fire and the smoky aroma, Dorus fetched the large saucepan from *la bête* and transferred it to a trammel hook in the barn and swung it over the fire to continue cooking. Charcuterie was laid out and the white wine gave way to a bottle of red *Château Vignelaure* as they chatted and warmed their burgeoning acquaintance in front of the heat of the grand fireplace.

"See that?" Dorus asked, pointing to the sky.

"What?"

"The shooting stars."

"Oh, wow. Yes!"

"If you keep watching you'll see hundreds. Thousands, maybe. I was told shooting stars are always there but you only get to see them in places where there is no pollution. Here, the air is about as clear as you'll ever get, so you'll see shooting stars all the time."

"Oh my God. Yes! I can see loads of them. Aren't you supposed to make a wish when you see a shooting star?"

"That's right."

"What do you wish for? Or aren't you allowed to tell?"

"Oh, that's easy. I don't mind telling. It's always the same wish. I wish I could go back in time and change everything so that I could be – well – normal. To make me whole. So that I could risk loving again."

"Can I have the same wish?"

"Be my guest."

"Then I wish to change my past too so I can be normal. Can I wish for it every time I see a shooting star? Can I wish it a thousand times over?"

"I do. But nothing ever changes. I just stay broken."

"Perhaps if we wish together."

"Worth a try. We must never give up hope."

Dorus and Anaya continued their communion by sharing wishes, hopes, wine and dinner before Anaya spoke with some angst.

"Dorus. You are very quiet. I've just found myself wondering what you are thinking about but I'm trying not to ask you."

"Nicely asked, if I may say so."

"Thanks. It took me a while to come up with that line. Well?"

"And you are right. We agreed to share our feelings and not hide things. So ..." Dorus' face creased to indicate his reluctance. "All it is, is that – well, do you remember me saying I was struggling with song writing?"

"Yes."

"Well, all my songs have been about betrayal, broken love and lots of shitty stuff like that. Turns out my misery sells well. But I'm just not feeling that angry at the moment. The fact is, travelling with you has been great." Anaya resisted the urge to interject and allowed Dorus another pause. "The fact is, for the last five years I've been telling myself how happy I am living alone. You know, no one to answer to; I can do what I want when I want. But I think I'm having to re-evaluate all that now. Maybe I've been lying to myself all that time. Maybe being with someone is actually better. And if it is, then what the hell am I supposed to do about it?"

"Sorry – my fault!"

"No, my fault. When I accepted the burden five years ago, my Burden Giver just paid the bills and let me get on with my journey. But what I've done here is set off on a road trip with you and found myself sharing your journey."

Failing to find anything to say as she tried to assimilate the significance of what Dorus had said, Anaya let his words hang in the air between them and meld with their shooting star wishes. Dorus stirred and reached down to one of the leather-bound notebooks which were never far from him.

"Bloody hell, Annie. There's a song right there. *Travelling together on separate journeys*." He scribbled lyrics into the pages and dropped the notebook back onto the floor with an exhalation denoting satisfaction.

"I hope you are going to give me credit for that one, Dorus."

Anaya's words met a smile from Dorus and the intensity of the night air laden with their darkening talk thinned as quickly as it had coagulated, but Anaya was compelled to continue what Dorus had begun.

"Actually, Dorus, there is something I've been thinking about too. Can I tell you?"

"Of course. Go on."

"Well, over the years, my coping strategy has been to bury myself in work to blot out anxiety, flashbacks, panic attacks and stuff like that."

"Yeah. I totally get that. I've been the same."

"But here I am. No work. Right out of my comfort zone. Loads of time on my hands and - and no flash backs. No panic attacks."

"That's good, isn't it?"

"Very good. But I don't understand it."

"We are a right pair of messed up nutters, aren't we?"

"Yup, we are. Where's a shrink when you need one?"

Before the threads of their confusion could begin to entwine, Dorus' mobile phone buzzed incessantly demanding his immediate attention.

"Oh, my God, I know who this is."

Dorus answered the phone and, in animated French complete with flaying arms and descriptive hand-gestures, he began a conversation during which Anaya heard her name repeated several times leaving her burning with something which may have been anticipation but felt more like anxiety. Finally, Dorus ended the call with tones of salutation and beamed at Anaya.

"Well, guess what. We've just been invited to lunch!"

"What? Where? Who by? No way! How come?"

Before answering, and to raise Anaya's curiosity even further, Dorus strolled past her and pulled two blankets from a chest at the back of the barn after tossing large pieces of wood onto the fire. He handed one to Anaya and swaddled himself in the other.

"Let me explain. After I first bought this place, I stayed here for a good while whilst the improvements were being made. It was falling down. Well, actually bits of it had already completely fallen down. I was pretty much camping for months. Anyway, I used my time productively. I actually wrote a whole album on that trip! I spent a small fortune getting this place to how you see it now but I made a hundred times as much selling the album. I did a lot of walking and on one occasion I found myself sharing a stretch of road with this guy called Sacha. We just got talking. Turns out he and his partner, Raphaël, own a little restaurant over there on the other side of the valley. They used to work in a posh Parisian restaurant together. Two Michelin stars! They fell in love and got together but they got a whole load of prejudice and abuse for being gay. They managed to get enough cash together and ended up running their own restaurant. They got a Michelin star there too. But working under pressure from early morning until late at night seven days a week was just about killing them. So, they sold up and moved here for the good life. They now farm a smallholding and use all their produce to cook the most amazing food for the little restaurant they run over there. They've got a little vineyard too." Dorus' eyes gave directional context to his words. "Sacha saw our lights on from across the valley and figured I was here so gave me a call."

"Wow. Amazing story. I reckon there's another song there too."

"Already done! It's one of the songs I keep for myself. I'm not sure why, but it was too personal to share. It is a very happy song I called *Accidental Harmony*. Except I wrote it in French, so it's actually *Harmonie Accidentelle*. Funny that I choose to keep a happy song but sell all the miserable ones. Anyway, I eat there whenever I can. They have kind of adopted me as their surrogate son. They know a bit about my past and kind of look after me when I'm here. They like to try out their new recipes on me. They refuse to let me pay so we've agreed that I donate money to *Enfants et Développement* instead - which is their favourite charity. It supports children in need in France but around the world too. It's a win, win, win."

"Incredible! And we are going there?"

"I told them I'd check with you first, but you'd be mad not to take up the offer. I should warn you that you'll be expected to eat and drink anything and everything they give you. No choices."

"Count me in! When are we going?"

"Day after tomorrow."

"Great. I'll starve myself ready for it."

"Er, no! We are in Provence. We will eat a lot and drink a lot and love every second of it - a lot."

"OK, if you insist. I reckon I can do that."

Dorus tapped a message out on his phone; the date was sealed and they relaxed by the dying fire.

"Dorus, talking of charities, do you remember when we were in Faulty Towers you said that you'd started a charity and that it had all gone wrong? You said you were going to tell me about it."

"Oh, yeah. Sorry. I forgot. Well, in a nutshell it took a year of my life and tons of cash and it crashed without trace. I set up a charity to build a hospital and school along with some housing in Africa. Loads of poverty and almost no healthcare there. Turns out our beloved country isn't too keen on offering that sort of thing. I got the project going and then I had a visit by three grey men in even greyer suits. They showed me ID and claimed they represented the UK Government. They said I was doing more harm than good. They said if I went ahead there would be a stampede of millions of people trying to get there which would create a humanitarian crisis. They also said my money was actually being hijacked and going to terrorist groups. They also told me that if I didn't stop, they would stop me. They scared the shite out of me."

"Christ. So, what happened?"

"I took the cowardly way out, of course, and stopped. I lost all my money. To this day I don't know if those guys were for real, but I'd obviously stepped into something nasty. Being

101

cynical, I wondered if it was all to do with foreign aid and deals attached to it. Maybe even arms deals."

"I'm not sure you are being that cynical there, Dorus. So, anyway, the end of your charitable work, then?"

"Sort of. Well, I donate to charities, but I still have a yearning to actually start something. If you have any great ideas that is another thing you might consider doing."

"Right. I'll put 'run an international charity' on my to-do list then as well as redesign your Cornish house and completely reconstruct my life."

"Excellent. You've got it in a nutshell. I'll hold you to that. Just don't look down."

The warmth of their smiles met the red ambers in the last of the fire and, after allowing the events of the day to settle as they emptied their wine glasses, they made their way to their beds which offered instant sleep to the exhausted travellers.

the voyeur

As dawn broke, shards of light pierced the cracks in the shuttered bedrooms and instructed Anaya and Dorus to begin another day. No sooner had the light begun to mellow and bathe the isolated cottage that hung like a watercolour painting on the side of the valley, the warmth it brought began carrying with it the lavender perfumed, valley air.

Coffees not teas were brewed on *la bête* which was now refreshed from its nocturnal torpor with finely seasoned wood. The conversation, like the heat in *la bête's* belly, was slow to resume but was warm, comforting and reassuring of the day to come.

"I'm going to hit that wood pile and start chopping it up this morning. What do you think you might do? Walk to the summit?"

"Yes, I think I will. I'll go exploring. How long will it take?"

"About an hour or so there and an hour back with as long as you want to sit at the top. A word of advice, though. There's no shade up there and it's going to get very hot. If I were you, I'd head off sooner rather than later and be back here for a late lunch before the sun really gets too unbearable."

"Perfect. I'll head off after breakfast. I'll take my phone in case I get lost."

"By all means take your phone, but you'll be lucky to find a signal. But you can't get lost. There is one path up and the

103

same path down. It really is that simple. If you are not back by this time tomorrow, I'll go looking for you."

"You'll come looking for me after I've frozen to death at night, then? Comforting thought, Dorus."

Their mutual succour allowed them to share a communal grin.

Dorus placed four croissants in the hottest of *la bête's* ovens and more coffee was poured allowing further discourse.

"What do you think about doing something with the chicken we bought for dinner this evening, Annie?"

"Me?"

"Well, I didn't mean that. I'm happy to cook. Do you like cooking?"

"Yes, I do. I love cooking. It's really cathartic."

"I know what you mean. Buy nice ingredients, chop them up, cook them and then eat it with a nice bottle of red. What's not to like?"

"Exactly."

"What's your signature dish?"

"To be honest I haven't cooked seriously for ages. We tend to look after ourselves in the house-share and cooking for one in the chaos of what passes for a kitchen is a bit difficult. My housemates don't seem to think it's real food unless it is served by Deliveroo. But if I could choose to cook something it would probably be Chicken Karahi. My mother was a great cook. I learned loads from her. Before she buggered off back to Lahore, she and I used to do all the cooking. I was very close to her once. Before ...."

Dorus' heart somersaulted as Anaya again began to regress to the darker places in her soul but instead of offering support, he picked up the threads of the conversation about cooking as a diversion.

"Sounds wonderful. As you can see, it's a bit basic here but when we get back to Cornwall can you cook it for me?"

"Yes, of course. I'd really love to. I miss cooking."

"Great. Can't wait. My kitchen in Cornwall is pretty well stocked, but when you get there have a look around and anything I haven't got we'll get in."

"Will do. I'm actually really look forward to cooking for someone. How about you? What's your signature dish."

"I don't really have one. I'm a bit eclectic. I'll see a dish or maybe eat in a restaurant and then I'll kind of cook on that theme. I've even been known to see a food dish on a billboard and then go home to replicate it. I just really like buying stuff in – especially fresh from a market - and then just laying it out until I decide what to do with it. Very limited skill but lots of enthusiasm. Cooking for myself always guarantees I have an appreciative audience."

"It sounds like we might have fun in the kitchen together. We could take it in turns to be chef and sous-chef."

"I'd like that. And don't laugh, but I always play music when I'm cooking. I find the type of music I listen to really influences how I cook."

"So, am I right, then? You start by choosing a wine, then choose the music and from that you create a dish?"

"Er, yes. When you put it like that, I do sound a bit nuts."

"Not judging, Dorus – just saying. I'll try it for myself when we get to Cornwall."

The croissants were pulled from *la bête* and eaten steaming with yet more coffee. Both Anaya and Dorus felt calmed and comfortable with each other as they put breakfast behind them and faced the morning before them. There was some mutual comfort in knowing that they would be separately engaged in different enterprises that morning thereby mitigating any need for further exploration of their neonate relationship.

"Right, I'm going to finish getting up and then head off up to the summit. Is it OK if I hog the shower?"

"Yup. No problem. I'm going to start chopping. I get a tad warm when I'm wielding the axe, so I'll take a shower later when I'm done. It cools me off as much as anything. I usually use one of those showers outside." He raised his arm in the direction of two outdoor showers which were hidden from Anaya's view at the side of the cottage.

Dorus began organising the woodcutting arena that he had previously signposted was to be the focus of his visit to the cottage and Anaya began organising herself ready for her solo expedition to the summit. After Dorus had sharpened his axe on an antique, foot-powered grinding wheel he positioned a sizable pile of timber ready for cutting as Anaya reappeared wearing a light, floral, cotton dress, light canvas shoes and fashionable sunglasses on top of her head nestling in her mane of hair.

"Good look, Annie, but you look ready for a stroll on Islington Green rather than a hike up a mountain."

"Oh, is this not right for the walk to the summit?"

"No, I'm joking. You look great. Maybe I'd dump the canvas shoes though and wear something a bit sturdier for walking. And have you smothered yourself in sunblock? And take lots of water."

"Yes, mum."

"Sorry, am I being a bit bossy?"

"Totally. Actually, though, I haven't put any sunblock on and I haven't got any water. So, thanks. And what the hell was I thinking of with these shoes? A little bit of the old 'towny-Annie' just took hold of me."

Anaya disappeared again into the atrium of the cottage whislt Dorus began wielding his axe and sending logs and splinters flying across the yard at the side of the house. Anaya reappeared with her face and arms now glowing with oily sunblock and with a shoulder bag stuffed with two water bottles and an apple.

"Do I pass inspection now?"

107

Dorus paused his assault on the woodpile to survey Anaya who was now wearing heavy Doc Marten style boots which shrieked contrast to the lightness of her dress. A contrast, Dorus thought, that was singularly comely.

"Yes. Good look and practical, Annie. Who'd have thought a cotton dress and army boots would go so well together?"

Anaya allowed a coy giggle as she accepted what she chose to believe to be a compliment and Dorus turned his body to ready himself for more axe wielding before bidding her to leave him to complete his task.

"Enjoy. It's a lovely walk. Not too steep and a great view. Where are we now – about 10 o'clock. So, an hour there, and an hour back with a good sit down – I'll expect to see you about twelve thirtyish. Let's aim for lunch at one, but its only charcuterie, cheese and fruit, so take your time. It'll wait for you if you take a bit longer."

"Great. See you later. I feel a bit guilty leaving you to do all the work, though."

"Don't. I enjoy it. Besides, it's your turn tomorrow."

"Don't make jokes – I'm definitely up for it."

"You're on. For now, just go and enjoy the view."

Anaya shrugged her shoulder to balance her bag, swivelled on her heels, slid her sunglasses from on top of her head down onto the bridge of her nose before leaving Dorus who was already decimating the next log.

As she climbed towards *le trône,* the sounds of iron on wood became dull and melted into the cacophony of insects signalling to each other from their clandestine hides. Remembering the sheer delight of sitting on *le trône,* she broke her journey with a visit there and soaked in the spectacle that the world offered up to her as she relived the experience of closing her eyes and becoming one with nature. As she sat alone her mind drifted away from work, away from jobs, away from her traumatic past and it directed itself towards an unknown future but one which was calling like a siren signal imploring her to embrace it. Even so, ripples of discomfort ran disconcertingly across her skin as she tried to accept the uncertainty of what she had committed to.

As before, time became meaningless and an hour passed before she felt cause to check her watch. At that moment, she decided that watch-wearing was for the old Anaya and that time was no longer to be her marshal. She undid the bracelet and dropped the now meaningless timepiece into her bag.

Concluding she would save the ascent to the summit for another day and perhaps do it with Dorus, she chose instead to return to the house and to offer help with the task of wood cutting. Her slow descent brought the sounds of Dorus' labour back into her consciousness and soon the idyllic cottage came into view some short distance ahead of her. Seeing a small copse, she wandered into its protective shade and found a tree stump on which to rest and to absorb the view of the stone cottage with cotton wool tufts of smoke emerging from its chimney, the yawning barn, the endless beauty of the valley and Dorus methodically cutting wood and stacking it with unnecessary precision. Time again began to meander past unnoticed as she continued to watch what she considered to be a poetic scene like something from a beautifully filmed movie. Dorus paused and pulled his sweat-sodden shirt over his head, rubbed sweat off his face with it and cast it aside into the dusty courtyard. He took hold of a water bottle, swigged deeply and emptied the rest over his face allowing it to flow down his semi-naked torso. Anaya tingled as the scene unfolded like a beautiful cinematographic canvas.

Yet more time ambled by lazily and Anaya thought she should leave the seclusion of the copse and announce her return, albeit far earlier than had been scheduled. But her intent to disclose her arrival both to the cottage and then to Dorus was abruptly halted and frozen as Dorus downed his axe, strolled over to the showers which were alongside the house and stripped naked. His movements were routine and casual but to Anaya the sight of his naked body was paralysing. He turned the tap and stood under a stream of icy water allowing it to wash away his sweat and to cool his overheated frame.

Anaya was transfixed at the sheer beauty of the scene. Dorus slowly rotated to ensure the water found every part of his body and then raised his arms and rested his head backwards to meet the downward torrent. Anaya told herself to look away. She told herself this was wrong. She continued watching.

She imagined she was there with him and that they were sharing the beauty of the *al fresco*, cleansing water. Being naked with a man was something that Anaya had avoided since the trauma of being raped; but now the raw beauty of the scene beckoned her to abandon her reticence and to embrace the liberating freedom the Provençal hideaway laid out for her. Watching Dorus became a beacon of freedom to her, commanding that she join him in order to shed the life-limiting inhibitions she carried.

She willed herself to join him but stayed motionless and transfixed.

Dorus reached out of the shower to find a bar of soap and began washing from his hair to his feet before again rotating slowly to wash the suds off and into the dust. Finally, he stilled the flow of water, took a towel and walked to the edge of the courtyard overlooking the valley to dry himself roughly before raising his arms again to allow the sun and the warm breeze to complete the task. Having dried, he stood motionless, staring into the far distance of the valley and of his life, communing with nature until eventually he turned, walked lazily back towards the cottage and, unbeknown to him, directly towards Anaya. Her bile rose in fear that she might be discovered and exposed as a voyeur, but Dorus barely raised his eyes as he disappeared into the cool behind the thick stone walls of the cottage emerging moments later wearing just a light, cotton kaftan. Having concluded his task for the day he pulled out one of the two reclining chairs, located it in the shade by the barn, lay back and closed his eyes.

Anaya, now confused and disorientated by her voyeuristic behaviour which, although not intentional, had not been averted, waited until her scheduled arrival time and then joined Dorus.

"Hi, Dorus, did I wake you?"

"No, I was just resting. I've been running through some lyrics in my head all morning. That Monet exhibition in Paris really got to me. Those paintings were amazing. I think I've got a new song coming in my head - so different to my usual stuff. I'll jot my thoughts down in a bit before I forget. How was the walk?"

"Brilliant. It's all just breath-taking."

Anaya tried to convince herself that she was not lying and deceiving Dorus, but she knew she was. She had promised to be honest with him and now she was breaking that pledge - and breaking his trust. She hated herself for how easily and unnecessarily her lies had formed. She had to divert herself before her self-criticism became self-loathing.

"Shall I bring lunch out?"

"Great. Thanks. I'm a bit knackered. I'll just lie here and be waited on."

Anaya walked into and out of the cottage in silence collecting charcuterie, cheeses, fruits and a baguette before arranging them with circumspection on the trestle table in the barn. Once the task was completed, she called Dorus to join her and lunch was eaten in relative silence. Dorus was recoiling from his morning's labours and Anaya was recoiling from the ugliness of the deceit she was now enduring and which was leaning on her like an unwelcome judgement being handed down by the pulchritude of the environment.

The afternoon was spent sheltering from the heat and the sun whilst Dorus periodically scribbled in his notebooks and Anaya hid behind her earphones listening to music to drown out her guilt whilst her mind rehearsed narratives which would allow her to confess her crime and thereby recover their relationship and her self-respect.

As afternoon began to close, Dorus announced he would begin preparing the chicken with some shallots and red wine. Relief temporarily visited Anaya as she found herself alone until Dorus eventually reappeared with the half bottle of white wine left over from the previous evening.

"Fancy taking this up to *le trône*?"

"Yeah. Great."

Dorus followed Anaya up the track and through the rock crevice and they both settled on *le trône* to share a glass of the ice-cold white wine. Anaya kept conversation to a minimum for fear of revealing the secret which now tortured her. Whilst sitting on *le trône* had hitherto been experientially cathartic for Anaya it now burned her as her secret burrowed its way through her conscience. The supernatural power that had previously enchanted her now chided her.

Dorus closed his eyes to commune with the valley but instead found focus on Anaya's emotionally taut aura.

As the sun relaxed its heat they returned to the cottage, Anaya laid the trestle table ready for dinner and Dorus completed the cooking over the now flaming fire in the barn. The synchrony of their movements reflected a newly formed and accepted routine but masked the coldness between them. Conversation was mute and functional and the evening air cooled further to match the unspoken gelidity between them.

A bottle of red wine was opened and drunk with the *coq au vin*. Conversation continued to be numbed and Dorus had let his anxiety rise because of it. He removed the dinner plates and returned with a selection of cheeses and another bottle of wine which he uncorked and placed down with unnecessary bluntness on the table as a signal he was about to make forceful demands.

"OK. Sorry, Annie. Maybe I'm just paranoid, but you've been off with me ever since you came back from your walk. Have I said something? Have I done something? Because, if I have, I'm really sorry. But this silent treatment is really doing my head in. Tell me. For Christ's sake, tell me what it is."

Anaya had never witnessed Dorus exhibit anger before and his display of ire forced her instinctively to retreat into deceit.

"No, nothing's wrong." Her lie bit her tongue and scratched her throat. "You haven't done anything."

"Are you sure? Then what is it?" His tone had calmed to that of a sympathetic parent.

"Yes, I'm sure, nothing's wrong."

Her second lie bit deeper, cracking her deceit and letting the truth fire itself out.

"Oh, shit. I'm sorry. It's me. I've ruined everything. I'm so sorry. I've really screwed up."

Pressure visibly welled behind Anaya's eyes as she grappled with words which might release her from her self-imposed guilt.

"What the hell could you have done, Annie? All you did was go for a walk. How could you have possibly done anything wrong?"

"I didn't go to the summit. I only went to *le trône*."

"OK, well, that's fine. It's not a hanging offence. So?"

"Then I came back and sat in that little copse just up behind the house. It was cool there and it all looked so beautiful."

"Again, I'm not going to throw you out for that. I know where you mean. I sit there sometimes too. It's a lovely spot. I'm glad you found it. So, what am I missing here?"

Anaya had become distraught and her tears had begun to escape their hiding place.

"You don't understand. You don't get it."

"Well, that's true enough. You are going to have to help me out. Look, just calm down. Don't cry. Please, whatever it is, we'll sort it. Just tell me."

"I watched you chop wood. I watched you!" Her voice had become sharp and shrill.

"Right. Now you are freaking me out. I haven't a clue why you are so upset. Yes, I was chopping wood. You knew that. So how did that upset you?"

"I watched you. You chopped wood and then you – you had a shower." Anaya's body slumped with the relief that she had finally said the words that had gnawed away at her all afternoon.

Dorus paused ruminatively to consider the meaning of the confession.

"And? I'm still not getting it. Here, have some more wine. Take a breath and tell me what's going on." Dorus filled her glass which she left untouched and he handed her a tissue from his pocket.

"I watched you take a shower. I sat and watched you. I was basically hiding in the copse spying on you in the shower."

Relieved, Dorus began laughing.

"Is that it? Is that what's been upsetting you?"

Anaya's eyes shot fire at Dorus as she responded angrily.

"Yes. Don't laugh at me! Don't you dare laugh at me! It's been cutting me up all day. Stop laughing!"

Dorus controlled his laugh and spoke empathetically as though calming a child that had fallen and grazed its knees before correcting himself lest he had inadvertently adopted a patronising tone.

"I'm sorry. Yes, it's cruel of me. I didn't mean to laugh. But I'm not laughing at you. I promise. I'm just relieved it isn't something serious. I thought we'd been getting on so well. I was beginning to think perhaps it was all too good to be true and maybe you were going to tell me that you'd had enough of me and wanted to head back to London."

"You aren't mad at me?"

"No, not in the slightest. Why should I be mad at you? Look, bodies aren't anything special. Especially mine. We've all got one. My view, for what it's worth, is that nudity in the right place is normal. I don't know. Maybe swimming, saunas, Jacuzzis, sunbathing - you know, that sort of thing should be normal. OK, so we don't live in a society where any nudity is acceptable, but maybe it should be. Anyway, it's me that should be apologising. I should have been more careful. I wasn't thinking. But I really did think you would be gone for at least another hour. I always shower out there normally. I'll be more careful in future. My fault, Annie, not yours. How could you have known I was going to take a shower?"

"You're definitely not mad at me?"

"No, not in the slightest. I should have thought about it before having a shower out there. After living on my own for so long I think I just take *al fresco* showering for granted."

"Are you sure? I thought I had blown the whole road trip and knocked the Burden Giving thing on the head. But it all looked so beautiful. It was a real Lady Chatterley's Lover moment. And I don't mean that in any pervy way – it was all just so beautiful."

"Well, maybe I spoiled the view a bit. I don't think I've ever been called beautiful before. But no harm done. I'm glad you've cleared the air. Now just relax. Have some wine and cheese. I just need to pop to the loo."

"Thanks for being so understanding, Dorus."

"Don't be silly. In fact, you should try it."

"What?"

"Try using the outside shower. Until you do you can't understand how natural it feels. The sun, the view, the air on your body. It just feels so right up here. I mean, don't if it would make you feel awkward. But if I make myself scarce and promise not to sit in the copse and spy on you, you should give it a go. I promise you; you wouldn't regret it. Not trying to be corny, but there is something really spiritual about it."

"OK, I will. I'm so sorry I bottled it up. You are right, being honest and open stops misunderstandings. I'll do better in future."

"Don't worry. We are all human. Now, I really do need to get to the loo before I pee myself."

Dorus got up and began making his way to the cottage but then, suddenly, turned and ran back extorting wildly.

"Shit, shit, shit! I'm being a total unfeeling git, aren't I?"

"What? How come? You were just really understanding."

"You seeing me naked. Was it triggering flashbacks? Oh God! I can't believe I could be so insensitive. There was I banging on with some homespun psychobabble about nudity and you were all cut up with flashbacks."

"Oh, God, no. Seriously. Not that at all."

"Promise?"

"Promise. To be honest - and *please* don't laugh. I've never seen a naked man before so it was kind of a big moment for me."

"What? But you must have done, you were …."

Dorus just stopped himself treading all over her trauma before Anaya relieved him of his sentence.

"*Raped* is the word you are looking for, Dorus. No. I'm knocking on twenty-five and I've never seen a naked man. When I was going to make love with my boyfriend, I was eighteen and that would have been the first time I would have seen anyone naked. Instead, I got a bag put over my head and got gang banged. I've never been near a man since – well, until you stripped off in front of me this afternoon."

"Oh, wow. How can you sound so flippant about it?"

"It's either that or get hysterical and go into meltdown, so count your blessings that flippancy wins."

"OK. I'll just try to be more careful in future. Sorry."

"You really must stop apologising for something I did. Anyway, like I say, you should do whatever you normally do. I shouldn't spoil it. And yes, I'm going to try showering outside too. You are right. It's natural. I've got to face my demons. I need to learn to be comfortable with my body."

"I know it's getting a bit heavy here, but I really am going to pee myself if I don't go to the loo. I'll be back in a minute."

Having completed his visit to the lavatory he re-joined Anaya with a relaxed look on his face, raised his glass to hers and made a toast.

"Here's to our *bumpy* journey."

"To our *bumpy* journey. It wasn't planned, but I think we covered some ground today."

"Yes. A journey worth travelling, I think. Potholes and all."

"I'll drink to that too. To the potholes in life. Cheers."

Dorus began secretly rehearsing some lyrics in his head about 'potholes in life' and Anaya began, now happily, reimagining the day's events.

"So, Anaya, tomorrow. I'm chopping wood again in the morning and I'll give loads of notice before I have a shower. Then, over to the other side of the valley for the best lunch you will ever have."

"Brilliant. Can I help do the wood too?"

"Are you sure? Don't think you have to. We can take it in turns chopping and stacking if you really want to. It will take half as long."

"I'll look forward to that."

"And at some point, we'd better turn our minds to heading back across France to Cornwall via Versailles and Giverny. Maybe we could sit down and do that tomorrow too."

"Great. You know, Dorus, I'm still struggling to come to terms with the fact that I'm doing all this."

"Well, you are, and you are doing it very well."

"Thank you kindly, good sir."

Emotional equilibrium and friendship were restored and transported them to a peaceful sleep after wine, cheese, shooting stars and wishes closed the day.

*****

The already crystal sharp morning light, the smell of freshly brewed coffee and of baking croissants filled Dorus and Anaya with the sense of contentment uniquely afforded by the familiarity of a newly formed routine.

"You still up for chopping this morning, Annie, or have you come to your senses?"

"Oi, you! Don't underestimate me. I'm not a frail little lady. I'll out-chop you any day."

"Challenge accepted. I reckon we'll get through that pile this morning. Then I'll put my axe away until next time."

"And I'm going to do the *Full Monty* too – take an *al fresco* shower."

"Good for you. I promise not to watch."

"Actually, I have a question about that."

"The water? It's just cold – no hot water outside, I'm afraid. Bloody cold actually. Straight from the spring as nature intended. It's freezing but beautiful."

"No. I noticed there are two showers. It just seems odd. There's only one of you. Why two showers?"

"Ah, that. Well, I don't really have an answer. Actually, it's worse than that. When you get to Cornwall, you'll see I have *his and hers* sinks in my en-suite too. Actually, come to think of it you probably won't see my en-suite. But if you did, you'd see two sinks. A double shower in there too. And two showers by the pool. I don't know why I designed it that way. My best guess is that very deep down I long for a partner to share all this with. But, as someone who can't ever have a partner, it all seems a bit stupid. But there we are – no accounting for stupid, eh? I tried to rationalise it once by saying it would increase the value of the property when I come to sell. But since I'm never going to sell it was a bit of a lame excuse."

Anaya felt the moment to ask about the reference to a pool had slipped by too fast and had been subsumed by darker references. Instead, she disarmed the potential to be drawn into their traumatic pasts again.

"Well, it means you'll always have a spare, then."

Her smile gave permission for the conversational thread and for breakfast to end and for the day to proceed. They changed ready to begin the task of splitting wood, the sounds of which were soon punctuating the immense calm of the rolling lavender fields and vineyards beneath them. The woodpile shrank and the wood stack grew proportionally until both Dorus and Anaya paused for rehydration from their water bottles.

"You aren't wrong, Annie. You are really strong. A bit demonic with that axe, if you ask me."

"Strong in many ways Dorus! Christ, I'm hot."

"Me too."

Dorus took the opportunity to drag his shirt off his sweaty torso which clung and resisted the unveiling. Anaya reached forwards to assist his disrobing by pulling his shirt over his head.

"Do you mind if I take my top off too, Dorus? Don't worry, I've got a bra on." The giggle that followed her request begged the only answer possible.

"Of course. No problem."

Anaya re-enacted the disrobing that Dorus had led leaving her wearing a fulsome sports bra, baggy cotton shorts and her large cumbersome boots with thick socks rolled over the tops. Dorus allowed just a fleeting moment to admire how perfect she looked despite modelling completely uncomplimentary items of attire and he had to push further thoughts away before they allowed him to begin analysis of his admiration.

"Right, Annie. Final push. We'll be done in an hour and then we can clean up and have a break before heading over the valley for lunch. We're expected there by about two so there's no big rush."

"Great. You know, Dorus, this is a perfect day. Some physical activity and a meal out. It couldn't be better."

They resumed their methodical tasks swapping every now and again between wielding the axe and stacking the logs. As the undertaking came to its inevitable but welcome conclusion, Dorus collected a brush to complete the project by sweeping away the splinters that had evaded immediate capture. These he stored as kindling in a bin originally designed as an animal food store.

"Right, Annie. All done. Are you still up for a shower? If you want, you can go first. I'll make myself scarce. Then I'll go second."

"Yes, I'm up for the shower experience, but I've been thinking. You will probably think this is nuts – and of course you can say no – but why don't we take one shower each and shower together?"

"What? Really? Well …"

"I know. Don't say it. But somehow, I think I'd feel less exposed with you there. I know that doesn't make any sense. I can't explain. Anyway, I totally trust you, plus I've seen you as nature intended already, so no shocks there."

"Well …"

"Sorry. No. I'm nuts. You are right. Stupid idea. Forget I ever said it."

"No. I was going to say – well, if you are sure, then I think it's a lovely idea."

"Really?"

"Yes."

"OK, then. Let's do it."

They each began running water through their respective, neighbouring showers and silently discarded their sweat sodden clothing whilst meticulously avoiding glancing at each other. Anaya stepped under one shower and yelped as the icy, spring water hit the warmth of her body and Dorus stepped under the other sucking in air to stifle his urge to exclaim his empathy.

They began to choreograph the rotations that the showers demanded, washed with soap and roughly dried using fresh towels. Dorus moved to the same spot Anaya had observed him stand the day before and she followed. They stood allowing the warm air to cool their damp bodies whilst looking at the expanse of the view and inhaling the expanse of the aroma. Dorus' right hand relaxed by his side and

Anaya's left hand relaxed by hers. Just inches away from each other, their hands passed a silent, unnoticed thought between them.

"You are right, Dorus. It's just perfect."

"Yes. And sharing it made it infinitely more perfect."

"Dorus, I don't think I know who I am anymore. This is so unlike me. Maybe I'm just so far away from my old life I can move on now."

Dorus found few words to demonstrate his understanding.

"Maybe it is this place."

"Maybe. Maybe it's this place and maybe it's you. Maybe it's both."

The smile that followed cemented the safety zone they had agreed without the need for verbal affirmation.

After their communion with nature and with each other had found a natural conclusion, they turned and headed for the cottage entrance and to their bedrooms where they dressed before regrouping in the shade by the barn. They reclined their tired bodies and sucked on water bottles until rehydration allowed further discourse as Anaya broke the easy silence.

"That was a big moment for me, Dorus. I still can't quite believe I did that. It's so unlike me. But …. but I just wanted to prove something to myself."

"You don't have to explain and you don't have anything to prove. I get it, I think. I think I was kind of proud of you. It must have taken guts. I was really flattered."

"Flattered?"

"Yes. I was flattered how much you have come to trust me."

"Hm. I guess so. Well, I crossed a bridge there. I knocked down a barrier. I'm proud of myself."

"Good for you."

"To be honest, Dorus, my heart was pounding. I hoped you couldn't see my shaking. I was panicking a bit at first, but when we stood side by side looking across the valley, I suddenly went all calm. I wanted that moment to go on for ever. That was the first time I had felt good about myself since I was raped. Then, when we turned around to go and get dressed, I suddenly felt really naked. You might have noticed me run a little bit to get inside."

"I must admit I was totally surprised when you suggested showering alongside me, but I thought you were just so cool about it. You must be really good at hiding your feelings."

"Yes, I am. I've had lots of practice."

"Me too. Sad, isn't it?"

"What do you mean?"

"Well, carrying a trauma around in your head and not having anyone to share it with."

"Oh, yeah. Definitely. I've never really had anyone to offload onto. Maybe Ruth a bit."

"Remember what I was saying about how living on my own is a good way to stay away from people so they can't hurt me? Well, the other side of that coin is that there's no one there to talk to either. Bit of a double-edged sword."

Anaya paused as though wondering if she should speak and then plucked courage from the words swirling in her head.

"Dorus. You know you can always talk to me, don't you?"

Dorus turned his head to Anaya and allowed his gaze to melt, momentarily, into hers.

"Likewise, Annie. Any time."

Neither dared accept the offer, but stored the thought in an easily accessible part of their minds.

The long and thoughtful lull that followed was challenged as Dorus pushed the day's events aside to make way for the next item on their itinerary.

"So, Annie, we've got about an hour or so and then we'll need to head off for lunch."

"How do we get there? Drive?"

"Well, this is a bit awkward. There's a battered up old Lambretta in the shed. Did you see it?"

"The old motor scooter? Yes, I did."

"Well, we're going to be drinking a fair bit today so I really don't want to drive, but buzzing along the dust track on the Lambretta somehow doesn't seem so bad – even though I know it is."

"Nice logic, Dorus. So, we'll go scootering then. Is *scootering* an actual word?"

"Well, it's definitely a word now. You OK riding pillion?"

"Yes, of course. Well, actually, to be honest I've never done that before but it sounds a doddle. Don't I just sit there and hang on? When do we leave?"

"In about an hour and a half. Come to think of it, there is a little village near the restaurant just before we get there. Shall we call off there on the way? It's a really cute place. Totally frozen in time."

"Sounds good."

"OK. So, off in about forty-five minutes then. Long enough to put your glad rags on?"

"Oh, are we dressing up?

"No, sorry. I was joking. Casual."

"Phew! I'll just finish this water and then I'll get ready."

Anaya swigged the last of her water and stiffly dragged her aching limbs into the bathing coolness of the air behind the thick stone walls of the cottage. Dorus pulled the aged Lambretta out of the shed, checked the fuel and fired it up to reassure himself it would still serve them. After both he and

Anaya had chosen clothing cool enough for the intense heat of the day they reconvened and eyed up their transport.

"Oh, Dorus, I think I have boobed. I wasn't thinking. I chose this full-length cotton dress because it is quite smart and it'll keep me fairly cool. I wasn't thinking about riding pillion."

"Not a problem. Ride side saddle. Just don't fall off. Hang on to me. I'll take it carefully. It shouldn't be a problem. Don't change, you look great."

"OK. I'm game. Let's try it."

Dorus handed Anaya a helmet and he donned his.

"Two helmets as well as two showers, eh?"

"Yes, I know. Don't let's go there again. Here we go. Just shout if you don't feel safe."

"You do know this helmet will wreck my hair which I've just spent ten minutes brushing, don't you?"

"Er, no, I didn't think. Hang on, sit here and trust me. I'll sort your hair out. It'll only take a minute."

"Seriously, Dorus? Are you actually offering to do my hair?"

"I certainly am. I'm a man of many talents. I grew up with a house load of girls next door. I sort of became an honorary girl until I started to sprout hair on my face. Come, sit. I've got some elastic bands inside."

"Don't you dare use elastic bands in my hair, Dorus. It's just not chic. I've got some hair bands in my bedroom. I'll grab them."

Anaya returned wearing a wrist full of hair bands and Dorus brusquely wove Anaya's thick, dark hair into four French braids.

"There. All done. Not bad for a rush job if I say so myself. I'll do them more carefully for you when we get time."

Anaya stepped towards her reflection in an old wavy-glass window to admire Dorus' hasty attempt at a suitable coiffure for both the Lambretta ride and the Michelin starred lunch.

"You really are a man of many talents. I like it. I don't know why I don't wear it like this all the time. It'll look after itself. Thank you kindly, Monsieur Sassoon."

"No worries. Any time. Now, helmet on. Let's hit the road."

Dorus straddled the front seat and kicked away the stand holding the scooter steady for Anaya to mount. Anaya carefully arranged herself on the rear seat and grabbed Dorus' shoulders tighter than was comfortable for him and he commanded the Lambretta into life with a flick of his foot. Slowly at first then with unrestrained abandon they headed down the dusty, lumpy track. Far from shouting with fear, Anaya whooped her exhilaration encouraging Dorus to push the Lambretta to its limit. The Lambretta met the challenge as though celebrating its liberation from its storage and Dorus and Anaya united in a shared memory of Ruth telling them to ride life like a rollercoaster and, for the duration of the wild descent at least, they discarded memories of the past, abandoned thoughts of the future and lived a moment of time in the present.

Ruth's commanding voice carried them on. *"Both of you just ride life like a roller-coaster and let it thrill you."*

For those brief, halcyon moments they did just as Ruth had bid them.

the restaurant

Like a tired, recalcitrant packhorse, the Lambretta summoned enough power to meet the challenge of the onset of the ascent on the other side of the valley but complained of the load it now felt as the road began to rise. Eventually, the vista of a cluster of houses, a café, a church and a handful of shops came into view.

"Here we are." Dorus rested the Lambretta on its stand alongside the lichen encrusted wall of the churchyard and both he and Anaya removed their helmets and shook their heads free from their incarceration.

Dorus swallowed dust in his throat before offering the inevitable solution to the combination of heat and dryness.

"Shall we grab a beer at the café?"

"Great idea. Can I have a quick wander first?"

"Sure. Go ahead. I'll get a table. What do you want? I'll order for you. Beer? Wine? Coffee?"

"Beer. Same as you if that's what you are having. Whatever. I don't mind. Just something to wash the dirt track out of my mouth. I'll just be five minutes. It's so cute here. I just want to take a quick look around."

"Beers it is then. I'll just be over there outside the café. See you in a bit."

Dorus made his way to a vacant table at the café on the edge of *La Place du Chapelle* and Anaya drifted away to explore the serenity of a Provençale village barely surfacing from its *faire la sieste*. Dorus joined the tables of tan-stained, leather-skinned, elderly men supping on their pastis and sucking on their Gitanes and Gauloises. He hated inhaling other people's stale cigarette smoke, but somehow the smell of French cigarettes intertwined with freshly brewed coffee and pastis was an intoxicating combination. A redolence that can only be found in French cafés and which dyes the air with a compelling charisma.

A waiter, hugged by his black apron and clutching used coffee cups destined for their return to the kitchen, appeared deferentially and Dorus ordered a small and a large, cold beer before correcting himself and changing the order to two large beers. He had come to learn that Anaya quite rightly regaled at the idea of assuming any sort of diminutive, female gender stereotype.

The beers arrived after an extended period of time designed to amplify his need to feel the first rush of pleasure as it hit the back of his dust-encrusted throat. Anaya was some distance off as he sat and watched her approach with her braided hair hugging the contour of her head and her cotton dress drifting in the breeze and swaying gently with the rhythm of her lazy steps. Her eyes seemed distant as she soaked in the details of the stone buildings and the age-stained walls which had long since lost track of time. Although she knew Dorus was sitting directly in her path, her demeanour gave a sense that she was simply alone. The gentleness of her gait gave the appearance of a hovering

134

apparition as she floated towards the group of male admirers who had temporarily abandoned their pastis and their conversations in order to focus their amour on Anaya as she approached, unaware of the appreciative eyes which scrutinised her.

Dorus smiled to himself whilst watching the gnarled faces of his café companions as their eyes fixed on her. Their animated communication stopped, allowing them to imagine they may have some connection to the visitant progressing towards them. Anaya reached the scene and sat next to Dorus who now beamed his pleasure.

"What are you smiling at, Dorus?"

"You totally owned that street, didn't you?"

"What are you talking about?"

"I think you might have a few new admirers."

"Who?"

"Oh, just everyone here. They couldn't take their eyes off you."

"Shut up. Don't be ridiculous."

"OK. If you say so."

Dorus allowed another smile to conceal the fact from himself that he had bristled with pride as it was he that she had joined at the café and that his neighbours must, he thought, have envied him. Anaya took hold of the condensation-drenched glass in front of her and gulped her first taste of

135

beer, leaned backwards and tilted her head to embrace the rush of coldness in her throat and the heat of the sun on her face. With her eyes closed Dorus once again allowed himself to drink in the perfection of the mirage sat beside him. Their drinking companions abandoned their imagining that Anaya might become a new lover and returned to their pastis, their cigarettes and their muted conversations punctuated with cackles of animated laughter. Time begrudgingly progressed as the village stood still until Dorus announced it was time to head off for what was billed to be a gastronomic feast. He paid the bill and strode towards the resting scooter.

Remounting the Lambretta now seemed routine and the puff of blue-grey smoke and the oily smell seemed reassuring as they left the village in its time-capsule and clattered the ten minutes it took to lift their lives into another dimension. As the worn brakes squealed in protest, Dorus brought their aged steed to a standstill and rested it on its stand. Anaya took in the scene. A larger than necessary two storey stone building with a garden bound by a low wall in front of it housing half a dozen wooden tables and dividing it from the mirror image of the valley that she had learned to love.

"That's us over there." Dorus gestured at nothing in particular on the other side of the valley but which Anaya understood was the general direction of his cottage.

"I just can't get used to this view, Dorus."

"Nor me. It's why I keep coming back. Well, that and everything else about this place."

Before they could exchange further exultations, a six-foot tall, round bodied, ruddy faced man wearing a blue striped apron with a cloth tucked into its waist bolted out of the house and headed towards them like an elephant released from captivity. Grabbing and squeezing firstly Dorus and then Anaya, his words gushed into the air, filling the space between friendship and acquaintance. He pulled them into the garden and gestured to a table laid out with four place settings, several wine glasses to each placement and two bottles of red wine. The flow of French facilitations broke momentarily as the apparition disappeared into the house and reappeared with a mirror image of itself.

"Anaya, may I introduce Sacha and Raphaël?"

Anaya quickly calculated correctly that it had been Sacha who had hugged her almost inappropriately yet harmlessly and that it was Raphaël that was now undertaking a performative bow and hand kiss whilst both of them simultaneously maintained a torrent of French salutations. Dorus did his best to keep up some sort of translation but failed.

"I think we are to sit here, Annie. They'll be joining us to taste their new creations."

Dorus' smile to Anaya was disarming as they took up their seats and whilst Sacha and Raphaël bustled around a handful of other guests who had clearly finished their lunches but were reluctant to leave. Having taken their seats, Sacha joined them and filled wine glasses with abandonment twisting the bottle with each pouring to prevent any escape of the precious, red nectar. He swigged on his wine and

137

rolled his eyes in praise of the Chateau Simone he had selected in honour of his guests. Raphaël had returned to the kitchens to finish preparing what was to be the first of many dishes leaving Sacha to verbally embrace his audience. Dorus kept up his attempts to provide simultaneous translations as dish after dish with accompanying wines appeared with theatrical embellishment and gustatory enthusiasm.

Anaya found herself falling in love with the two animated Frenchmen and with the generosity of their hearts which they served along with their inventive and inspirational cuisine. Each course was described with enthusiasm and punctuated with lip pursing and hand gestures which made Dorus' translations almost redundant. They had found a common language as they consumed and embraced the feast, the ambiance and the genuine comradery.

Hors d'oeuvres of goat cheese crostini with fig-olive tapenade, zucchini fritters with shallots and pancetta tortilla crisps were followed by an amuse-bouche of finely sliced beetroot chips with braised fig and caviar. Caprese bites with basil vinaigrette and a pea soup served in a shot glass were produced next and each mouthful teased the pumpkin sage bisque which followed and which gave way to broccoli with shishito peppers, pickled onions and mushrooms stuffed with Pecorino Romano, garlic and bread crumbs. A garden salad of lettuce, tomatoes, onions and tart vinaigrette refreshed their palates to welcome grilled salmon with a soy sauce marinade and a liquorice and star anise foam.

"It's the first of the main courses next, Annie." Dorus grinned at Anaya. "I'm not joking. We haven't got to the main course yet."

"Great, I'm really peckish." Anaya almost slipped over her words as she matched Dorus' grin.

Roasted duck with an orange-ginger glaze arrived next and which paved the way for deep-fried turkey with a honey bourbon drizzle which in turn demanded a palate cleanser of lemon sorbet and prosecco to prepare for herb-crusted venison medallions.

Only a short pause was allowed before cheeses were presented with accompanying jams, chutneys, spicy mustards, caramelized onions and candied pistachios.

Fruit tarts with a champagne mousse teased a sense that the finishing line was not too far off but miniature butter madeleine biscuits, small pieces of bitter chocolate and bite-sized macaroons all served with coffee and brandy eventually signalled the satisfactory conclusion of the gastronomic marathon.

Despite the number of dishes, each with its perfectly matched accompanying wine, neither Dorus nor Anaya felt overwhelmed. The rapidity of the constant stream of French conversation, however, had been completely overwhelming. Dorus had diligently maintained an ongoing translation and Anaya had been duly included in discussions of the finer points and critiques of each dish as it was presented, sampled for olfactory satisfaction, consumed and admired.

As the extravagant alimental theatre came to a close Dorus, Sacha and Raphaël chatted together but Dorus ceased his ongoing translation. Anaya heard her name repeated and noted Dorus' body stiffen in an increasing display of embarrassment. Both his tone and his body language betrayed his discomfort leaving Anaya side-lined until it was time to leave and to endure the inevitable but welcomed hugs and cheek kisses.

Dorus handed a helmet to Anaya, fired up the waiting Lambretta and they headed back through the village and towards their valley-side home. After a few minutes, Dorus pulled off the main track a brought them to a standstill by a meticulously kept vineyard. He dismounted and tugged his helmet off as he slumped down in the shade of a solitary tree and invited Anaya to join him.

"Phew, that was something wasn't it? Can we just rest here a while whilst I get my breath back? Well, I warned you! What did you make of it? Brilliant, eh?"

"Yes. It was amazing."

"You sound a tad underwhelmed! I thought you'd love it."

"No, the food was out of this world, the wines all beyond belief and those two guys are larger than life and made in heaven. I think I just fell in love with them a bit."

"Why the grumpy face then?"

"Nothing."

"Don't give me that. We've been here before, Annie. Out with it."

"Well, you did a great job translating. Thank you for that. But, but ...."

"Go on. Whatever it is, just spit it out."

"Well, at the end you deliberately stopped translating and I heard my name over and over again. If you were talking about me, I think I deserve to know. Why did you stop translating?"

"Oh, that. Yes. I'm sorry. I should have translated for you. I was embarrassed."

"Why?"

"You don't want me to tell you."

"Actually, Dorus, I do want you to tell me. No secrets, remember?"

"Look. They are who they are. They mean well. There's nothing in it. They were just talking."

"OK. Now I'm freaking out. Tell me now or I'm walking back."

"It's a long, hot walk back to the cottage, Annie."

"Walking back to London! Just tell me. What was so awful about me that you stopped translating. Didn't they like me?"

"They absolutely loved you, Annie. Genuinely. They thought you were perfect."

"So? What's so bad then that you can't tell me?"

141

"Oh, Annie. Must I?"

"You so must, Dorus. Just spit it out before I punch you!"

"Right. Here we go. Just don't read anything into it, OK?"

"I can't promise. You've managed to build this up into something important now. Just tell me or I really will punch you in a minute if you don't!"

Dorus drew breath and looked away to avoid Anaya's eyes and to avoid the rising embarrassment which was retarding the pace of the words forming in his chest. Eventually, the words lined up into staccato sentences and he braved sharing them.

"Right. They said that you and me make a very handsome couple. They said our babies would be drop dead gorgeous. They said that we had to invite them to our wedding and they said they would kill me if I didn't ask them to do the catering. They also said that they wanted us to bring our firstborn to the restaurant for a celebration of their first grandchild."

"Grandchild?"

"Yes. I told you they had adopted me. They treat me like the son they will never have, so our child would be their grandchild. Please don't be angry."

"Angry? Why would I be angry. Well, actually, yes, I'm angry. But not because of what they said. Because you weren't going to tell me what they said. What happened to honestly and openness?"

"Yes. Sorry you are right. I was just embarrassed."

"Why embarrassed? What they said was beautiful. Who knows, in a parallel universe all that might come true one day. Where's your romance, Dorus?"

"Hm. I think my romance got a bit nobbled some years ago. I'm sorry. OK?"

"You are forgiven – but only just. Not telling me just fuelled my paranoia. Anyway, shall we get back? I feel a snooze under the stars coming on. Plus, we have to sort the next bit of the trip, don't we?"

"Yes, indeed we do. I'm sorry if I spoiled a good day."

"I should think so, Dee."

"Dee?"

"D for *dunderhead*."

"Fair enough."

"Come on Dee, my carriage awaits. Take me home."

With some relief, Dorus coxed the Lambretta with its two charges back to the cottage where both it and they sighed in satisfaction at the successful completion of their journey.

*****

With no fire in the barn to heat them and to keep the coldness of the evening at bay, the warmth of *la bête* invited them to spend the remainder of the day inside the cottage interrogating Dorus' laptop in order to find a course for the next segment of their journey.

"I'm really sorry about what they said, Annie."

"You can't apologise for what other people say, Dee."

"Still calling me Dee?"

"Yup. You are always going to be Dee from now on just to remind you what a dunderhead you are for not talking to me. Consider yourself bollocked and don't do it again."

"Guilty as charged, Annie. If it is any consolation, I feel a bit stupid now."

"So you should, but you are forgiven. No more secrets, OK?"

"OK. Changing the subject quickly, I was just wondering about extending our stay a bit before we head home. How do you fancy a quick trip down to the Med? Maybe head down to Cannes for a day. It takes about two and a half hours to drive there so what if we drive down and have a quick stop in a hotel?"

"That would be absolutely amazing. Yes, please! Are you sure? Do you have time?"

"OK. Yup. I'm not under much time pressure. I do have a deadline to come up with some songs, but it's a while off yet and I've got lots of notes to work on so, let's do it then. One night in a hotel down at the Med and then back here for one more night before we head off. In the meantime, let's book up our return trip."

Dorus tapped at the keyboard until they settled on a hotel on the seafront in Cannes and then another half way to Versailles. They then proceeded to book tickets for a visit to the Palace of Versailles and to Giverny together with a further hotel situated between the two. More tapping on the

144

keyboard brought the booking page of Brittany Ferries into view ready for the final leg back to the UK and onwards to Dorus' Cornish cottage which would indicate the end of the road trip and the beginning the true purpose of their journey. Both knew, but didn't need to voice, the significance of their ultimate arrival in Cornwall. It would be the moment in time when The Burden would transition from Dorus to Anaya.

"Right, Annie. There's room on the night crossing so we can book that. Shall I book one cabin or two. It's just bunks to sleep in overnight but if sharing a cabin makes you feel awkward, I can book two. It's not a problem. Whatever you want. It's the Pont-Aven which is a really nice boat. It has some big cabins. Maybe we could book one of those – or two if you want."

"No, one's fine. I've never been on a ferry before. I think being on my own at sea might freak me out a bit. Especially at night. We can argue over who has the top bunk!"

"Fine. I'll book one big cabin. They are much nicer. So, that's it then. We head for a night at Cannes tomorrow and then back here for one more night and then, when we are all done, we'll head across France. For me that means heading home."

"You know, Dee, I'll genuinely be sad to go."

"We can always come back."

"I hope so. I'd like that. I hope me being here was OK for you. I know this place is very special to you."

"Having you here was great. If I'm brutally honest, it surprised me a bit. I can hardly imagine being here on my own again now."

"Well, if I'm invited again, I'll definitely come. You know, I can hardly think about living in London now either. It's really odd. It's like I'm discovering a new me. I wish I knew what my future held, but I hope it includes a return visit here."

With all aspects of the next and final steps of their road trip now finalised, they wandered outside into the chill of the night and wished wishes as they stood gazing at the pyrotechnics the shooting stars presented to them like a gift from the universe. As the shooting stars appeared, slid across the sky and disappeared again, they each wished the same wish but without sharing it. This time they did not wish to change their pasts, but to change their futures. Neither were aware of what their futures held and neither had yet formulated any sort of plan. The two travellers felt at the mercy of something that was unfolding around them but which chose to withhold its secret from them. Being there together in that moment sufficed to give them hope.

a chorus in cannes

Before setting off after an early breakfast, Anaya reminded Dorus of his offer to do her hair for her when they had time.

"So, Dee, if we have a few minutes do you fancy braiding my hair again? I really like the look on me."

"Yes, no problem. Just hang on a minute. Sit there, and I'll be straight back."

Dorus scuttled away and ferreted through what he described as his *girl-draw* and returned carrying several yarns of coloured thread.

"Dee? What the hell?"

"Well, Annie, even a bachelor has to be able to sew. Actually, especially a bachelor has to be able to sew. Just sit still and trust me. You are going to like this - maybe. I can always take it out if you don't like it."

After spending several minutes longer than was necessary brushing Anaya's hair whilst she concealed her winces, he began methodically creating six tight braids each with coloured threads interwoven into them like rainbows. When he finally finished, Anaya sought a mirror inside the cottage, emerging within seconds.

"Dee. For God's sake. It's beautiful. I actually look like a different person. More to the point, I feel like different person."

"Well, I like it too. I can take it out if you want. Have I gone too far? I'm afraid I rather got carried away."

"No. Perfect. I love it."

"Great, come on, let's head off."

Dorus aimed the Audi downhill and shimmied along the winding, dusty track until they met metalled roads and eventually began cruising along the *route nationale* heading south.

"You look happy, Annie."

"I am. I'm happy as a bird. I feel free. In fact, I feel like I am homeless which would once have scared me to death but now just makes me excited. And, if it isn't too embarrassing to say, I'm travelling with a friend. I haven't really had one of those for a very long while. I've not had anyone I was happy to call a friend for as long as I can remember."

"Likewise - on the friend bit. Anyway, settle down. About two hours to go according to the GPS."

"Do you know what is making me so excited, Dee?"

"What?

"You are taking me to the seaside. I feel like a little girl. This will be the first time ever I've been to the seaside. And yes, I feel ridiculous when I say that out loud. Nearly twenty-five years old and never been to the seaside. How sad am I?"

"You are easy to please, Annie."

"Well, stuff you take for granted is like an adventure to me. I've got so much catching up to do."

Dorus smiled a smile to himself content that he was the provider of his companion's happiness. He turned up the radio and fiddled with the cruise control before settling down to allow the Audi to assume command and to power down to the Mediterranean with minimal input from him. Anaya soaked in the beauty of the countryside as it slid effortlessly by under Dorus' stewardship until they eventually joined the coast at the *Avenue de Dr Raymond Picaud* along with a multitude of other tourists heading towards the *Vieux Port de Cannes.* Once there they found their hotel, the *Radisson Blu,* overlooking both the old port and the sea. Eventually finding a parking space after struggling against the endless queues of traffic Dorus stepped out into the heat with a howl of relief, stretched his back and looked up into the sun. Anaya followed but her excitement overshadowed her travel fatigue allowing her to absorb the new vista that met her.

"God, Annie, everywhere is so busy. And I hate to disappoint you, but this is hardly the seaside. I know that there is sea and sand here, but just wait until we get to Cornwall. There are lots of proper seasides there. We'll spend a day on the beach there and I'll buy you a bucket and spade. Oh, and I'll buy you a Cornish pasty for lunch. Not to mention a proper cream tea with clotted cream."

"Well, I think it's amazing here. So busy though! And those boats! Look at the size of them. Come on, let's have a wander."

Unable to check in until later that afternoon, they began exploring the port, the waterfront and the shops before they sat, *al fresco*, at *L'Assiette Provençale* enjoying a slow seafood lunch and a crisp glass of chilled *Chateau de Berne*.

"This is just so wonderful, Dee. Much more built up than I thought it would be, but it is still just so amazing. I just love it. Plus, drinking wine in this heat is going straight to my head. You might have to carry me back the hotel."

"I can't remember the last time I was here. I don't usually go to busy places like this, but yes, I'm really enjoying it. I suggest that after lunch we have another wander then check in. I guess we'll want to find a restaurant for this evening so keep your eyes open for something you fancy."

"This really is a great spot for people watching, isn't it? I'm making up stories about everyone. Like her over there. Look at her. All bleached hair and silicon. I reckon she is twenty-six going on sixty. Third marriage I reckon and made millions out of each divorce. She's had so much work she can hardly even sip that ridiculous cocktail she's got."

"There's a lot of that around here. It's the place to come and pose. Rich and body beautiful. This place is a testimony to the skill of endless plastic surgeons."

"Not sure I'm going to fit in, but it's still great fun."

Finishing their seafood preceded a more leisurely finish to their wine before they enjoyed a lazy stroll along the seafront both admiring and abhorring the wealth displayed in the rows of extravagant superyachts. They paused a short distance from a flamboyant marina watching a lone sailor trying to winch a life raft onto its muster station on a luxury yacht named *Isabella*. The growing frustration and impatience of the solitary seaman subliminally provided some gentle theatre as they progressed in no particular direction. The sailor pulled and pushed controls and the winches groaned and buzzed as the life raft began swaying uncontrollably. The actor in the rising drama became more and more exasperated until he finally called out to Dorus and Anaya.

"Hey. I don't suppose you can help me out, can you?"

Dorus stepped forwards.

"Yes, of course. We are just land lubbers so I don't know we'll be much help."

"Amazing. I promise you, there is no skill required. This is meant to be a simple job, but my deckhand didn't turn up so I'm struggling. I've just had her out on sea trials but I need someone to hang on to the ropes either end to steady her while I winch her back on board."

"OK. No problem. Just tell us what to do."

Dorus did consider this to be a problem but was driven by conventional politeness rather than reveal his reticence to become involved in this stranger's dilemma.

"Great. I'm Nigel by the way. I'm captain of this floating vanity statement."

"I'm Dorus and this is Anaya."

"Right. So, Dorian grab that rope there."

Dorus was used to being called Dorian and didn't bother correcting him.

"And Enya, grab that one."

Anaya was used to being called Enya and didn't bother correcting him.

"This shouldn't take long. She's got a bit tangled up in the rigging, but if you steady her, I'll untangle her and lower her down onto her berth."

The manoeuvre became lengthy, complicated and very hot as the sun rose to its height and then began lowering again spilling its intense heat onto the increasingly frustrated trio. Eventually the life raft sat in its muster station and Nigel began offering his undying thanks.

"Oh my God! I'm so sorry that took so long. I must thank you properly somehow. Are you on holiday?"

"Sort of. I have a place a couple of hours north of here but we are just visiting Cannes for the day."

"OK. Come on board. At least let me give you a cold drink to say thank you."

"No, no need, we are happy to have helped."

Anaya intervened.

"Please ignore Dorus. I'm not missing a chance to pose on the deck of this monster."

Not waiting for any remonstration from Dorus, Anaya began heading up the gangplank and found herself being ushered onto a reclining lounger on the deck. Dorus followed and Nigel disappeared below deck before reappearing with three stubby beer bottles. After twisting the caps off the bottles, he handed one to Dorus, another to Anaya and raised his in their direction. The rush of coldness on their palates dispelled the frustration of the past events as the three sat in the shade of a canopy. Anaya pushed her sunglasses onto the top of her head and slid down into her seat as though intending not to move again.

"Seriously you two. That was a life saver – no pun intended. Tell me, where are you staying?"

Anaya noted Dorus with his eyes closed apparently listening to the air and responded.

"Oh, over there at the Radisson by the old port."

"Nice. Quite posh, isn't it?"

"Don't know. We haven't checked in yet. But how can you say it is posh? Just look at this boat! This is posh personified."

"Yeah. Nice little rig. Not mine though. I'm just the hired help."

"The captain?"

"Yup. That's what they call me anyway, but I don't do much captaining. I sit here most of the time cleaning and oiling stuff. Occasionally I get to do sea trials, but otherwise I'm just a caretaker."

"How come you don't sail her much? Isn't the point of a boat like this to be sailed?"

"You'd think. It's the same with all of these superyachts. We just sit here most of the day. Most of the year, actually. They are tax right-offs for the super-rich. My boss is a dot com billionaire. I think he's only ever been on board about four times."

"What a waste."

"Total waste. Occasionally I'll get a call and then sail her off somewhere exotic so he can have cocktails with his rich mates. I rustle up a crew and sail her half way around the world and back just so he can have a bit of a booze-up to show off."

"Christ. It's another world."

"Tell me about it. Look, me and a few of the other captains are having a get together on board here this evening. Just a bite to eat and a few drinks. We take it in turns. It helps keep us sane. Why don't you join us? It's the least I can do to say thank you."

Dorus' eyes flicked open and his mouth began to form what Anaya thought might be a polite refusal before she interjected.

"Oh, that would be wonderful. Should we bring anything?"

"Nope. Just your good selves."

"Very kind." Dorus offered. "Right Annie. We need to get checked in. We'll see you later then, Nigel."

After disembarking the *Isabella* Anaya sought to placate the apparently moody Dorus.

"Sorry Dee. I shouldn't have jumped in so fast, should I? Don't you want to go?"

"I'm just not much of a party lover. But no, it's fine. It sounds fun. Come on, let's check in and then go for a stroll."

After checking in and finding their rooms, they set off for a walk along the opulent boutiques and casinos of La *Croisette* and on to the old quarter, *Le Suquet,* before heading back to their hotel to rest.

After readying herself for the evening aboard the *Isabella,* Anaya found Dorus waiting in the foyer of the Radisson raising a champagne flute to greet her.

"What are we celebrating, Dee?"

"Absolutely nothing. We are surrounded by riches and wealth, so I thought we should blend in. Besides, I think I was a bit negative about going to the *Isabella* tonight, so this is my way of apologising."

Anaya reached for her champagne flute and raised it to Dorus with a grin. They sat and gulped their champagne with fixed smiles.

"I could get used to this, Dee."

"Right, Annie, let's get it over with. Let's go partying on a superyacht - which is a sentence I never thought I'd hear myself say."

As they approached the *Isabella* Nigel waved to them enthusiastically and beckoned them on board where they were greeted by half a dozen or so of his fellow captains along with their body beautiful girlfriends and companions. Dorus subconsciously calculated the average age difference between the more elderly captains and the scantily clad, nubile nymphettes who were hanging on their arms and their every word.

"Everybody. Let me introduce you to my new friends. Dorian and Enya."

"Well," Dorus meekly corrected, "Dorus and Anaya, actually. But pleased to meet you all."

"Christ, I've been calling you by the wrong names all afternoon! So sorry."

"No worries. We shouldn't have such silly names."

"Speak for yourself." Anaya corrected.

A fellow captain who introduced himself as Peter took the opportunity to draw the new companions into their comradery after embracing Anaya and kissing her hand whilst somehow maintaining eye contact with her.

"Well, I'm Peter. A nice easy name. What brings you to Cannes? Are you sailors?"

"No, I'm an architect and Dorus is a musician. We are just passing through."

"Great. What do you play, Dorian?"

"It's Dorus actually. I write more than play."

"Sorry, Dorus. What? Classical?"

"No, pop."

"Brilliant. Would I know any of your songs?"

"Lots probably. They are on the radio all the time."

"Like what?"

"I can't tell you."

"What?"

"I'm a ghost writer so I'm afraid I can't tell you."

"What?"

Anaya completed the inevitable dialogue with her own intervention.

"That's right. He can't tell you. Oh, and I've just been sacked from my job."

"What?"

Dorus and Anaya smiled a knowing smile.

"Something tells me you've had that same conversation before." Peter joined their smiles and Anaya took up the mantle.

"Yes indeed. We are walking conversation stoppers, I'm afraid."

"Well. Good to meet you anyway. Here is an easy question. Fancy a beer?"

Both accepted the offer and Peter fetched an armful of stubby bottles and distributed them widely to the assembled party. Voluble conversation followed in an array of international accents but effortlessly in English as the nautical carousal gained momentum. Nigel produced crab cakes, fish tacos, tortellini & shrimp skewers with sun-dried tomatoes, smoked salmon devilled eggs and an assortment of breads and local cheeses.

"Wow, Nigel. This is amazing." Anaya spoke with genuine admiration.

"Thanks. We are all chefs as well as cleaners and captains. To be honest, we compete a bit when it's our turn to host. Anyway, look, don't be polite. Tuck in and grab drinks whenever you want them. No one's going to wait on you, so just grab what you want and relax."

Much grabbing and relaxing took place until a guitar was produced and the chefs-cum-cleaners-cum-captains took it in turn to lead the singing of sea related songs which demanded group singing of the choruses.

As Dorus soaked in the animated characters and the bonne amie which was being liberally shared on the deck of the *Isabella*, his attention was drawn by a diminutive, dark-haired woman who sat slightly apart from the hub of bodies. Her eyes were wells of darkness and she appeared to be scrutinising her fellow comrades. Her attire of brightly-coloured hemp wraps set her apart from the other female guests who had embraced their feminine wiles with tightly fitted, brief shorts and contour hugging boob tubes in order to snare their respective captains. He had longed to write something with more gravitas than the songs which had brought him riches. Perhaps, he hoped, an operetta. He had made a collection of memories of interesting and characterful people he had encountered or observed on his walks and his journeys in the hope that they might form themselves into some sort of storyline for him to describe in an operatic libretto. The image of the female enigma before him, whose name he ascertained was Roberta, but who responded to Bertie, imprinted itself in his mind for future use.

As the final chorus of the song led by the last captain in the circle came to its discordant close, Dorus steeled himself for what he knew was about to be inflicted on him. Nigel led the assault as he thrust the guitar towards Dorus.

"Hey, everybody. We have a professional musician on board. Come on Dorian. Give us a song."

"It's Dorus actually. Well, I don't normally …."

"Don't be shy. As you can see, none of us can sing."

"Well. OK, but I warn you. My songs are all miserable."

"I'll get more drinks. Off you go Dorian."

"OK. This might not work, but Anaya and I went to the Monet exhibition at the Louvre on our way down. I was struck by his paintings. It was not so much how he painted the flowers in his garden, it was more how he saw the flowers. It was as though he painted them like they were talking to each other. It was like he was eavesdropping on their conversations. Anyway. I've had some lyrics and some tunes running around my head ever since, so I'll have a stab at getting it out. Sorry if it all goes wrong."

"So, it's a world premiere then?" Peter chimed in.

"I guess so. In fact, even I haven't heard it myself yet."

Dorus first began to retune the already perfectly tuned guitar in order to steady his nerves and then began strumming a few chords before finding the notes to pick a series of arpeggios which gave the abused, wooden instrument a voice that it had never found before. His vocal introduction began hovering over the rapid flow of plucked strings forming a complex, contrapuntal form gently modulating around a perplexing array of keys. Firstly in common time then five four and back to common time, he allowed the tempo to increase and pause. He delivered first a crescendo and then a diminuendo ending in a transcendent suspension whilst his fingers ran a rapid conclusion to his story.

The throng fell silent and Anaya closed her eyes to see Dorus more clearly. To her he now became a series of complex and tortured layers desperately seeking to find serenity.

As the sentience of the plants in Monet's garden that he had conveyed gave way to praise and admiration from the congregation, Dorus rapidly returned the guitar before an encore was demanded. Immediately, his attention turned to Anaya who was being dominated by Peter leaning into her face with lustrous intent. He was repeatedly handling her shoulder and arms in accompaniment to his amorous and suggestive dialogue. Dorus felt his angst rise but was immediately distracted by one of the female guests who was similarly bronzed and wearing a loose, cotton wrap and displaying her cleavage which she was using as a weapon intended as a direct assault on him.

Once again, Dorus found the familiar feeling of fear embracing him and he turned to Anaya for help who, in turn smiled, nodded knowingly at her predator and stepped away from him to join Dorus.

"Well, Dee. I guess we should be going then. Long drive tomorrow and then we've got to pack up ready to head off back to England."

"Yes. Got to go. Thanks everybody. Great evening," chimed Dorus hurriedly.

They levelled their intent at the gangplank which signposted safety but, before either of them could escape the embrace of the friendship being showered on them, a slight woman with deep, wild, dark eyes and wearing layers of brightly dyed, swirling hemp cornered them. Her similarly wild, black hair swirled like a snake-haired gorgon as she obstructed their escape. Roberta had left the perch she had occupied all evening and had blocked their escape. She began urgently pleading with them.

"Come. Come with me. I need to read you. I can see your stories."

Despite their attempts to exit, the animated nymph-like apparition escorted them to the bow of the yacht and, with her eyes closed, began swirling her arms as though swimming through an invisible mindscape.

"You, Dorus. I can see pain. I can see you carry a great weight. But what's that? It's a box. I can see your box. Come with me. We must look inside. Come with me. We can look inside together. Hold my hand and open the box."

"No. Sorry. I can't. I just can't."

"Hold my hand. Come look inside."

"No. I've got to go."

"And you, Anaya, you too carry a weight; but it is you that holds the key to Dorus' box. You hold the key. You are the key. Dorus, the day will come that you will want to look inside your box. It will be Anaya's hand that holds you. You will be safe. You will carry each other."

"Sorry. We have to go."

Panic had grasped Dorus' chest as he scrabbled down the gangplank almost losing his footing and gasping for air as Anaya followed similarly deflated and confused.

Appropriate farewells were chorused as their new found comrades watched them disappear uncomfortably and they headed back to the old port and the safety of their hotel.

Dorus abruptly broke the silence and exhaled his words angrily.

"What the hell was that?"

Anaya, who was in her own emotional bubble, ignored Dorus' question and proclaimed her own exasperation.

"Effing git!"

"What? Sorry. What did I do? Did I say something? Was the song rubbish? Did I embarrass you?"

"Huh? No. I mean that effing git who was all over me. Effing Peter, I think his name was. He just about stuck his tongue in my ear he was so close. What a slimy creep."

"Oh, yes. I did notice. I wondered if I should rescue you."

"Nice thought, Dee, but let's be honest, it was you who needed rescuing. That skinny piece of tanned leather just about wrapped her tits around you. I actually thought you were going to faint at one point. I didn't know anyone could go that pale through a tan like yours."

"She was terrifying, wasn't she?"

"She was a bit. You didn't stand a chance. You certainly looked terrified anyway. And who was that woman doing the séance thing. Bit spooky if you ask me. Anyway, I'm knackered. Let's get some sleep. What's the plan for tomorrow?"

Dorus and Anaya chose to ignore the prophecy which had involuntarily been inflicted on them but instead stored the memory with an option for future inspection if emotional fortitude might allow it.

"Right. Shall we meet in the foyer at about eight and then walk along the front to find a café for breakfast? I reckon that would be nicer than a hotel breakfast. Then, I guess we can have a final look around and head off after lunch."

"I just love the way you navigate your days meal by meal. I've come to rather like it. Yes. Sounds great."

They separated to locate their respective rooms where Dorus lay in his bed wracked by the feelings of jealously he had encountered watching Anaya being verbally and physically manhandled. In an adjacent room Anaya also lay awake juggling her feelings of jealously having observed the amorous attack on Dorus.

*****

Morning brought a gentle stroll, a breakfast of coffee and croissants and a visit to the *Mairie de Cannes,* the *Château Thorenc* and the *Église Notre-Dame d'Espérance.* Lunch was a picnic on a small beach and their journey back to their hermitage on the side of the valley two hours away was undertaken largely in silent contemplation fed by physical and emotional fatigue. The events of the previous evening aboard the *Isabella* had troubled them both but neither could find the intellective capacity to analyse what had transpired and neither were inclined to share their disordered thoughts.

The arrival back at Dorus' cottage seemed routine. They exited the Audi and they both busied themselves independently until it was time to enjoy the evening with food and wine but one which was spent with subdued conversation about their plan for the following days rather than about the events of their immediate past.

After an eclectic supper intended to use up anything and everything not yet consumed, they retired to their bedrooms early and mercifully sleep took them both quickly and submerged them in regenerative cocoons until dawn offered them an early start and the chance to close one chapter and begin another.

crossing the line

The morning light commanded both Dorus and Anaya to *la bête* earlier than normal in anticipation of their imminent departure. Dorus had not fed *la bête* the previous night in order to allow it to begin its hibernation and the sun had not yet begun its lavish warming of the awakening air. The morning chill hastened their progress and Dorus had become anxious to leave the cottage and to begin their journey in order to avoid the possibility of any interrogative conversation.

"If it's OK with you, Annie, we'll head off sooner rather than later and stop for breakfast after we've put a few miles behind us."

"Yes, of course."

Neither wanted to leave but both wanted to begin the journey in order to leave the events of the *Isabella* behind. Partly due to their mutual desire to leave their hideaway and partly due to lack of coffee, neither felt the inclination to converse. However, rather than erecting a barrier, their shared silence continued to cement the blossoming bond they had accepted without intent nor contrivance. The need to exchange thoughts verbally had been replaced by a shared understanding.

They each showered using the remainder of the hot water, packed their personal belongings into the car and Dorus cleaned and primed *la bête* for the next visit, shut down and drained water from the pipes, switched off the electrical supply and finally checked all the windows and closed the shutters. Having completed the routine circuit of departure chores, he revisited each task in turn to ensure he had completed everything correctly before he finally delivered his leatherbound notebooks to the back seat of the car and announced that it was time to leave.

Firstly, they stood with their backs to the house taking in the morning light casting long, sharp shadows over the contours of the valley and then they turned and mournfully bid farewell to the cottage that had prised open fissures in their self-understanding, had offered no solutions but had bonded them and had secretly offered them some options. Both knew they had placed a foot into the safety zone that had shielded them and each was determined to use this departure to withdraw back to their individual and separate worlds.

The two ruminative travellers loaded themselves into the Audi and the engine hummed its acceptance at being woken. They signed off the events of the last few days and began a new focus on what might transpire over the next few.

Dorus found some neutral words to begin their descent to civilisation.

"After we've got out of the valley and onto the main roads we'll stop for a coffee. Is that OK?"

"Yes, of course. I can last a bit longer."

"The autoroutes are fine. There are lots of service stations but none of this part of the journey will be very exciting. It'll just be a means to an end."

"No problem."

For Dorus, the journey ahead was simply a chore but for Anaya it was a chance to soak in every detail that France offered to her. The fields, the buildings and the changing landscapes coloured in her perceptions of the world but most importantly it coloured in her perception of herself.

They stopped for coffees, croissants and petrol. They stopped for a baguette lunch and they stopped simply to rest from the endless tarmacadam. Finally, Dorus pulled the Audi into a parking space outside the *Hôtel de la Poste* in the town of Beaune and they unfolded their bodies ready to seek out the reception in order to announce their arrival.

The hotel, an understated but grand period building, had decorated itself with blossom trees in its courtyard and it presented a warmth to the travellers which welcomed them into its bosom. The gold lettering used to proclaim its name above the entrance suggested an important history and the green shutters framing the windows suggested that it was comfortable with its French heritage.

After checking in, they agreed to rest for an hour or so before heading out to explore what the town had to offer. Anaya arrived back at the reception area first having descended the grand staircase, momentarily allowing herself to believe she was someone important to the hotel. She had watched her image reflected in the wall-sized mirrors which had been carefully placed to allow guests to place themselves in the grandeur of the sweeping steps.

She stood on the chequered, tiled flooring surveying the high fenestration between the vestibule and a bar area. The separating barrier between the two areas appeared to have once been an outer wall. Her architectural analysis deduced that the vestibule must have been a courtyard but had been enclosed at some point to provide additional indoor seating.

She greeted Dorus as he made his entrance down the stairway towards her. The grandeur of the staircase appeared to concomitantly endow Dorus with some degree of grandness as he stepped methodically down step after widening step.

"Dorus, this is very cool. Have you been here before?"

"No. When I travel on my own I usually just power back to get the journey over with. Stopping here is a real treat."

"Come on. Let's explore."

They immediately embraced the opportunity to immerse themselves in the impending experiences which they knew would help them bury the troubled thoughts they had endured following the evening on the *Isabella*.

Beaune began spilling out its architectural splendour as they meandered around the narrow streets and cobbled communal areas which were littered with tables inhabited by animated characters enjoying the characterful ambiance, early evening drinks and the coolness of the weakening sun.

Anaya repeatedly paused in front of buildings inspecting details and enthusiastically describing their merit and their place in the evolution of architecture. Extravagantly coloured tiled roofs, decorative dormer windows and meticulously presented floral displays filled their senses and dispelled their travel fatigue. Layered on top of the grandeur and history that the town was not reluctant to display was the boast that this was the wine capital of Burgundy. At every opportunity parasols, shading crowded tables, proclaimed their proud wine heritage. Adding to the bustle, was an open market selling fresh produce from the region.

Anaya captivated Dorus with her infectious, detailed analysis of the *Hospices de Beaune*. She regaled him of how it must have been constructed, which wings must have been added and how it was 'literally an archetypal renaissance design'.

Both Dorus and Anaya soaked in the aromas, the sounds and the beauty of their *flâneur*.

After a brief return to the hotel, they revisited the town square now bathed in soft, yellow light from decorative streetlamps and café frontages and, after finding an available table outside the *Brasserie Carnot*, they leisurely consumed a typical regional menu. They mused that although both the Boeuf Bourguignon and Coq au Vin on the menu were regional recipes, since they had eaten both of these under the shooting stars of Provence, then they should extend their palates to sample other, alternative local delicacies. They chose Jambon Persillé and Lapin à la Moutarde to be accompanied and complimented by a full-bodied Burgundy. The richness of the wine contrasted with the mellowness of their conversation about places in the world they should visit and of how architecture and music were inextricably linked. Dorus had found genuine admiration for Anaya's knowledge and enthusiasm for architectural nuances and wanted to advance the assertion that there was a direct causal link with music which defined and shaped societies.

"If I remember correctly, during the renaissance period Burgundy was the home of pavanes and galliards. I can just imagine them dancing in some of these grand buildings around here whilst the lower classes danced the basse danse and the bransle in the town square."

"I'm impressed, Dee."

"Well, you might not be if you Google it and find I'm talking bollocks. Seriously though, I wish I knew more about architecture and music. It fascinates me how they go hand in hand in societies and cultures."

"Yeah, and yet most people walk around looking at their phones whilst *WhatsApping* their mates and listening to pop music on their AirPods." Quickly realising her derogatory reference to pop music, she added, "Oops. No offence Dee."

"None taken. I totally agree. So, when are you going to put together a must-see list of key buildings around the world for us to go and visit?"

"I'll dig out my final dissertation. It's all in there."

"Brilliant. I'm serious, by the way!"

Not knowing the degree of seriousness Dorus was intending, she raised her wine glass.

"Once more, Dee. To journeying."

"Together," responded Dorus.

Coffees concluded their meal and a final ramble through the evening streets watching lovers lazily stroll by in lockstep brought them back to their hotel and to deep and peaceful sleeps content that their friendship had become effortless.

An early breakfast and a meaningful departure set them back on course to their next resting place which lay half way between the Palace of Versailles and Giverny. Their hotel, *Les Tourelles de Thun*, was set in Normandy apple orchards and was built in 1888 by an architect called A Roussel. Anaya once again immediately began to enthuse about the neo-gothic construction which had been refurbished and redecorated by the heir of Raoul Rosieres who had maintained a classical modern style.

Anaya chose to accept the offer of pampering and indulged in spa treatments that the hotel provided whilst Dorus found seclusion with his leatherbound notebooks in the shade of an ancient apple tree in the hotel grounds.

A light supper and mercifully light discourse ended the day as they bid each other good night and sought much needed restorative rest.

The morning brought the two tired travellers to breakfast and then on to the next stop on their itinerary. The drive to the Palace of Versailles and finding suitable parking was tiresome and stressful for Dorus but fascinating and absorbing for Anaya. However, having reached the Palace, Anaya's passion glowed with descriptive enthusiasm for the magnificence which was unveiled before them and which raised Dorus' spirit. Anaya saw the building in different terms than Dorus, but his mind expanded to accommodate her perceptions. She lauded various architects who had contributed to the splendour and magnificence of the iconic structure. Louis Le Vau, Jules Hardouin Mansart, Charles Le Brun and Andre Le Notre all became names that flowed from Anaya's effervescent mind impressing and absorbing Dorus as he tried to keep up with the knowledge she imparted with infectious passion.

They walked the paths of endless historical figures as they captured the essence of past times of majesty and ruthlessness.

Pausing at intervals to redress flagging energies, they consumed convenience foods aimed at deceiving tourists of its nutritional value until both their spirits and their bodies found nowhere else to retreat other than back to the hotel in order to restore for the next day's exploration of Monet's life at Giverny. Minds and bellies were full and sleep beckoned them to early beds ready to begin again in the early morning.

Coffee, croissants, cheese and fruit provided fuel to start the day and the drive to Giverny was more pleasant and relaxed than the drive to Versailles. The queue to enter Monet's Garden was tedious and the heat was energy-sapping but the immediate perfume and colour which greeted them as they entered was overpowering. They shuffled amongst the

173

throngs of tourists pausing to photograph both the flowers and themselves and they bathed in Monet's ghost which was imagined in his house.

The colour-themed borders drew Anaya's eyes down and the trees and bushes drew her eyes up. The transcendent scent mingled with the riot of colours and textures and Anaya made a mental note to return again and again to observe seasonally induced transitions.

Both Dorus and Anaya paused for the longest at the Water Lily Garden which froze time and gave sapience to the bordering weeping willows, cherry trees, rhododendrons, azaleas, ferns and irises.

Anaya observed Dorus pause at regular intervals and close his eyes. She observed him slip a leatherbound notebook out of his pocket and scribble frantically whilst glancing around to ensure no one was watching. She saw him in a private world and she decided he should be left there until he chose to share it with her.

Eventually, as exhaustion drained them again, they sought a café to annul their fatigue. A late lunch expanded into an early dinner before they headed back to their hotel to enjoy mellow conversation over a bottle of soothing local wine.

"I'm loving this road trip, Annie, I really am, but I'm exhausted. I can't wait to get home."

"Me too, Dee. Albeit your home not mine. But I want this trip to go on forever. I feel like I have so much to catch up on. I've missed out on so much. Thank you again for bringing me."

"Thank you for coming. Let's just say that we brought each other. "

"Yes, I like that."

"Anyway, I'm hitting the sack early again. It's about six hours on the road tomorrow. It'll be your job to keep me awake."

"I'll do my best. I'm going to chill in the garden for five minutes and then head on up to bed. *Bon nuit*, Dee."

"Goodnight. See you at breakfast about nine. We are sailing overnight tomorrow, but we can board early and have something to eat and drink on board. I just need to sleep first."

Dorus lay in bed allowing the vision, the aroma but above all the narrative of Monet's garden that swirled in his mind to massage his imagination and to refine the song he had performed abord the *Isabella*. Later, Anaya lay in bed allowing her mind to interrogate what Dorus had experienced but had not yet communicated. She felt he had seen something altogether more experiential than actual and she was desperate for him to share it with her.

Eventually, exhaustion again gave both deep sleeps and gentle awakenings. Breakfast was lazy as the previous day still coddled their souls and the following drive was tedious but they eventually came to a merciful standstill in the queue to board the Brittany Ferries ship, Pont-Aven.

Arriving at the ferry port brought them to an anti-climax but one that was filled with nervous anticipation. Just over one hundred miles of water now separated them from the end of their road trip and the start of the next and most demanding part of their journey at Dorus' home. Hitherto, the matter of the burden had been a tacitly avoided subject, but they both intuitively knew it had to be voiced on the other side of the water.

Passport and ticket checks took them to another holding area and busy French staff in high visibility jackets chattered on walky-talkies before marshalling them and their fellow travellers aboard the waiting ship which was readied for departure. The weather had deteriorated with rain and wind nagging at an anxious Anaya who had withheld her true reluctance to sail overnight across the English Channel.

After boarding, they climbed the claustrophobically narrow staircase to their accommodation deck and navigated a host of directional signage to locate the deluxe cabin Dorus had booked. He had wanted Anaya to enjoy her first experience of cross channel travel in luxury but when they finally found their cabin amongst the endless narrow corridors of the cruise ship Dorus opened the door and exclaimed in horror.

"Oh, my God, Annie. I am so sorry. I've right royally screwed up. Look, it's a double bed, not bunks. Don't worry, I'll go to reception and get another cabin. There are bound to be some going. God, I'm so stupid."

Anaya entered the cabin, cast her eyes around inquisitively and then paused before retorting with some degree of uncertainty in her mind but with a firm, almost anxious tone in her voice.

"Oh no you don't. You are not going to make me stay in here on my own. I'll freak out. I wasn't looking forward to the crossing anyway, but the weather has really got up now. I'll brick it if I'm on my own. Can we work something out in here? I don't want to be on my own."

"OK, but what are you suggesting? There's only one bed. Maybe I could make up a bed on the floor or something."

"I can see there's only one bed, but it's massive. Look ...." Anaya began karate chopping down the centre of the bed to make a line in the duvet. "That's my side and that's your side. Just think of it as two bunks – just side by side."

"OK. If you are sure."

"Yes. I'm sure. It's the lesser of two evils. I'll be happier knowing you are there."

"Right, in which case, let's take a peek at the shops and stuff and then maybe a bite to eat and a quick drink if you fancy something before we turn in."

"OK. But I'm a bit worried I might be sea sick. Maybe a quick drink. I mean, you can get something to eat, but I'm feeling really churned up. Sorry, Dee."

To show empathy despite his nagging hunger Dorus agreed they would find a bar for a quick drink before settling into their cabin. They briefly explored the ship's expensive shops and shared a hurried drink in the noisy bar but tourists, school parties and lorry drivers inflicted discomfort on the road weary couple making relaxation impossible. Dorus drank his beer as though desperate for rehydration and

Anaya gulped her gin and tonic like others might down a shot of tequila. A brief nod to each other signalled that the tranquillity and serenity of their cabin would provide a sleep-inducive ambiance. They rose in unison and threaded their way through the cacophonous sonance of their temporary travel comrades until the hushed safety of their cabin welcomed their return.

On entering their shared space, they both eyed the bed cautiously but neither spoke of their reticence to share the privacy of their sleep as they allowed lassitude to conquer their natural inhibitions.

"It's tee-shirt and boxers for me, is that OK, Annie? I'll get changed in the bathroom."

"Don't be silly, I've seen you as nature intended – twice. So, I don't think a pair of boxers is going to freak me out." She felt her responses to be a lie, but the lie was to herself not to Dorus. "I guess I'll go for the girly equivalent, then."

Anaya readied for bed in the bathroom and hurriedly slipped into *her side* of the bed wearing a baggy tee shirt which hid her light, cotton knickers. Dorus likewise prepared for sleep and joined her. The ship's engines growled and rumbled as the propellers began their rotations juddering the steel hull.

Announcements over the ship's tannoy confirmed that they were about to leave the safety and calm of the harbour and further announcements informed the passengers of the procedures that must be adhered to in the event that the captain ordered the need to abandon ship. Seven short blasts and one prolonged blast on the ship's alarm system would denote the urgency for passengers to leave their cabins and belongings and to make their way to the nearest muster station ready to be given life jackets and to be designated a life raft.

"Christ, Dee. They really know how to put a petrified girl at ease."

"Really? Are you freaking out?"

"A bit." She meant, a lot.

"Honestly, Annie these ships are built for much worse than this. There's nothing to be scared of. The Point-Aven is huge and very stable. There's nothing to worry about, I promise you."

"I know. You don't have to tell me. Being rational isn't going to help."

"Don't worry. Just try to get some sleep. We'll be there before you know it."

Anaya was unsettled and unable to sleep for fear of the unknown and Dorus was unable to sleep for fear that Anaya was unsettled.

After less than an hour of the silence between them being drowned out by engine noise and the crash of waves on the hull, the Pont-Aven went about and the waves now slammed into the side of the ship before a new course drove the ship bow first into the oncoming storm causing it to suddenly pitch and yaw.

"Oh, shit. I'm sorry, Dee. Brace yourself."

Anaya slid across the double bed past the line she had scribed in the duvet and wrapped herself around Dorus.

"Christ, Annie you are shaking."

"Really? I hadn't noticed!"

"Don't worry. I've got you. Hang on to me. You'll be fine."

"I'm sorry. I feel just a stupid wimp. Can you just hold me for a bit until it calms down?"

Anaya clenched her face and rode the storm warmed both by Dorus' body and the ongoing reassurance he offered in gentle tones. The sea began calming as they eventually approached British waters but they continued their embrace until the ship sailed flat.

"Can I admit something to you, Annie?"

"What, were you scared too? Just too macho to admit it."

"Nope. Being scared was all yours I'm afraid, Annie."

"What then?"

"Please don't try to read anything into this. I'm just sharing, OK? But, well, I'd forgotten just how good it is to hug someone. I haven't hugged anyone since – you know."

Anaya wanted to reciprocate a reply which endorsed Dorus' confession but her words were blocked by the reality of what she wanted to say.

"And, Annie, hugging and chatting in the night. It's good. It felt good."

"Yes." Was all she found.

They had crossed the channel and had crossed a line. Both
knew it. Both felt it. Neither intended it. Neither spoke of it.

*****

Coffee, croissants, fresh orange juice and jams were brought
to their cabin and quickly consumed while the Pont-Aven
engineered a gentle docking manoeuvre despite the swell in
the port. Disembarkation was slow and the post-Brexit
immigration controls tedious after which the two sleep-
deprived travellers began the final leg of their road trip and
began the next leg of their now inextricably entwined
journeys.

home

The drive following disembarkation took a further two hours after fighting the early morning traffic through Plymouth and the endless tourist traffic arguing for road space along the main arterial road through Cornwall. Dorus struggled to stay awake during his tedious, routine drive and Anaya stayed curiously alert soaking in the Cornish countryside. They shared an extensive but repetitive conversation in silence as their minds examined their foreboding and their doubts of what lay ahead. The road trip had been an adventure filled with individual and shared exploration but the real journey, which had a real purpose, had not yet begun and had not been properly mapped out. They instinctively knew that they shared the same unclear concern and there was no need for them to articulate it.

Traffic worsened and ground to a standstill making the final miles tedious and exasperating but, finally, they began to approach the Pendeen lighthouse on the North Cornish coast of Cornwall. Dorus diverted the Audi away from the tourist routes and began navigating narrower and narrower lanes until the wing mirrors of the Audi brushed the foliage on either side and the high Cornish hedges which denied them views across the rolling hills and oncoming cliffs. Eventually, Dorus swung the car into an entrance closed off to them by a pair of imposing wrought iron gates. Sliding his window down, he placed his hand on a biometric pad which had been hidden behind an innocuous wooden cover and the gates doffed in acknowledgment of their master and granted them entry.

"Isn't that the same security thing like at Faulty Towers, Dee?"

"Yup."

"Seems I'm the only one who doesn't have one. I'm obviously an old fashioned kinda gal. I just have a key."

Dorus was too tired to engage but instead headed along the half mile, winding driveway edged by elm trees which crowded above them creating a tunnel until a two-story stone cottage with grey slate roofing and a small stone-built garage came into view. Other than a dilapidated shed, Anaya could see nothing more of the structures that Dorus had described to her.

Understated but rather grand was Anaya's initial assessment. Fitting, she thought, for Dorus. It created the feeling of splendour but which was to be secreted from prying eyes.

Having parked on the gravel apron and taken their belongings indoors, Dorus beckoned a coffee machine into life before temporarily retiring the Audi from service behind the garage doors.

"First things first, Annie. Let me show you your room and then coffee. Then I'll give you a guided tour."

"Great. Despite what you told me, Dee, this place is lovely. I'm happy to give it some thought, but it wreaks of being a home. We architects sometimes forget that being 'homely' is

183

often the most important thing we can ever create. You've got shed loads of that here. I'd hate to spoil it."

"Steady on, Annie. Let's take a look around first before you get to work – when you understand it then give it some thought. But thanks. I do love living here. It is definitely my home."

Dorus lifted Anaya's bags and she followed him up the stairs from the open-plan living area which, she thought, bore a singular similarity to the more expansive layout of the penthouse at Faulty Towers.

"That's my room and can I suggest you use this one? It's en-suite and has sea views. The other one is much smaller."

"This is perfect. Thanks."

"Right, settle in and I'll get the coffee going."

Dorus returned to the kitchen and, as Anaya followed moments later, she was greeted with the sounds of a coffee grinder and a rush of sharp, coffee aroma. Dorus completed his task of amateur barista and ushered Anaya to a seat at a dining table in a bay window where they sat, leaning on their elbows, watching the sea begin to find some degree of calmness after its ebullient night.

"OK, Dee. You definitely win."

"What have I won?"

"Do you remember standing at the window in Faulty Towers and you telling me how much you preferred your view of the sea? Well, I have to agree now. You were right. You can keep the city view. This is just magical."

"It's beautiful, isn't it? It never stops moving. Never stops changing. Never stops amazing me."

"It's wonderful. I'm in love with it already."

They drank their coffees and fought back the tiredness which nagged their bodies.

"Right, Annie. Where shall we start? In my dungeon?"

"Dungeon? That sounds a bit sinister!"

"It's surprisingly nice down there. Come on. Follow me."

Dorus led the way across the living area to a wooden door to the left of the kitchen area. He disappeared through the door and awkwardly descended a short, steep stairway flicking a switch on as he entered. The steps were narrow and shallow causing Dorus to almost sidestep in order to find a secure footing.

"So, this is the first design fail. Accessing the underground world via these steps is a nightmare. Look, here's my wine."

Dorus gestured with his arm and Anaya briefly noted two walls laden with wine bottles but her focus was on a large, thick, steel door which was left open and a new, wooden door now filling the entrance to another world. To Dorus' clandestine world.

Dorus pushed the door open and lights flicked on revealing a characterless, windowless corridor with one door directly ahead at the far end, two doors on one side and one door on the other.

"So, here is the useless room." Dorus pushed the single door open to reveal a small but well-equipped gym. "It seemed a good idea at the time. I did use it once."

"Like the ubiquitous gym membership, eh? You sign up and then never go."

"Exactly. I'm really embarrassed by it. Maybe we could do something better with it. Anyway, follow me into my secret world. Over here, through this door – my studio!"

Anaya followed Dorus into the most private part of his life and marvelled at a large space divided into two rooms connected by a door and a large glass panel. The first room was filled with instruments including guitars, keyboards and a variety of drums. Microphones and speakers interrupted the floor space at what appeared to be carefully choreographed intervals and cables littered floor spaces which should have been free for safe passage but which instead created multiple hazards. The second room housed an impressive mixing desk and an array of computer monitors.

"Wow! Dee! This is incredible. It's huge. Do bands come here to record stuff?"

"Nope. It's all mine. A bit over the top, isn't it? It kind of grew over the years. The more songs I sold, the more self-indulgent I got. You are the first person ever I've invited in. Sorry it's such a mess. Actually, you'd better brace yourself for the fact I'm going to spend quite a lot of time down here.

If I don't turn my scribbles into songs soon, I'll spontaneously combust."

"I'm duly honoured. Yes, of course you can hide in here. I'm intending to become your architectural sleuth, anyway. I'll be busy."

"Now you've been into my inner sanctum you'll have to come and make music with me! Do you sing? Do you play?"

"Yes, I sing – really badly. Actually, when I was younger, I used to play the tabla. I see you've got some." She nodded towards a pair of tabla alongside a sitar, a tanpura and a sarod.

"Brilliant. I'm crap at those. I'm trying to teach myself. I'm rubbish at them. Maybe you could give me a lesson. We'll come and play some time. Onwards. Next part of the tour."

Dorus led the way out of the studio far sooner than Anaya would have liked and turned towards the door at the end of the corridor.

"Excuse me, Dee, I think you missed a door."

"Oh, that. That's my dirty little secret."

"What?" Anaya exclaimed in a genuinely disturbed tone.

"No, I'm joking. It's nothing bad. Oh, God. Alright, I've got to show you now, haven't I?"

He turned around and pushed open the door. Lights flickered and he entered a windowless room to the hum of an air extractor and a musty, oily smell. Immediately, Anaya was reassured by the sight of the familiar Audi in which she had spent her journey with Dorus as they circumnavigated France.

"Hang on, Dee. So, the garage by the house isn't a garage?"

"No, it's just an entrance to that ramp over there. The garage is here underground."

Next, her eyes fixed on a light blue Mark I Austen Healey Sprite which she approached with an admiring stride. The overhead lighting showed off its seductive curves and the headlights stood erect along the lines of the front wings giving it an almost comical, froglike character.

"Oh, my God. She's beautiful. She's amazing."

"No, the *bug-eye* isn't my little secret. But yes, she is beautiful. I go joy riding in her on sunny days. She's my pose-mobile."

"I didn't have you down as a poser, Dee."

"Nor me. But she's irresistible. Anyway, she's not the secret. Look, over here. This is it."

He directed Anaya to a dust sheet covering another vehicle at the far end of the subterranean garage. In a single movement, he swept the dustsheet off and discarded it revealing a British Racing Green Aston Martin DBS Superleggera. Anaya gasped.

"Oh, dear God! I don't believe it! Can I sit in her?"

"Yes, of course. Just don't judge me. A quarter of a million pounds worth of total self-indulgence. I can't justify it."

He pulled open the door and Anaya slotted herself behind the walnut steering wheel.

"For someone who can't drive you really seem to appreciate a motor, Annie."

"This has to be my all-time dream of a car, Dee."

"OK, then here's a deal for you. When you pass your driving test, you can take her for a spin."

"Really? Seriously? It's a deal. I'll hold you to that. Actually – if I pass it first time can I take them both for a spin? The *bug-eye* and the Aston?"

"You drive a hard bargain, Annie. No pun intended. But yes. It's a deal. Sometimes I do the London to Provence trip in the Aston. So, if we do that road trip again maybe we could share the driving next time."

Anaya was too engrossed in the feel and the smell of the car to bother agreeing, but she secretly filed the suggestion that she might just have been invited on another road trip with Dorus.

"Right Annie, one more bit of the underground and then I'll show you around outside."

Anaya reluctantly extricated herself from the Aston Martin and followed Dorus to the end of the corridor where they paused whilst he flicked half a dozen switches housed in a wall mounted box with a grey, glass cover. They then entered a bright, carefully lit room smelling of ozone.

"For Christ's sake, Dee! A swimming pool! You never said you had a swimming pool!"

"Er, I think I did. I told you about the two showers by the pool." He gestured across to two showers standing between a Jacuzzi and a sauna.

"Well, yes. Two showers by a pool just doesn't say an Olympic sized swimming pool with a sauna and a Jacuzzi!"

"Hardly Olympic sized, but still, a swimming pool. Maybe I undersold it a tad."

"A tad? Really? Anything else, or can I just go into meltdown now?"

"No, nothing else. Well, just this, maybe." Walking around the far side of the pool, Dorus pushed another switch and large glass doors slid open onto a concrete patio with raised flower beds overlooking the sea.

"This is a bit of a suntrap. But you see the problem. An old stone cottage with some old wooden stairs which lead to all this via a cellar. It just doesn't work. That's where you come in."

"Yes. Once my pulse has come down, I'll give it some thought."

"Anyway. Let's head back up. I think we need a chill day after all our travels. Maybe we could come for a swim and a sauna before dinner."

"Brilliant. What about outside? Can you show me around out there too?"

"Sorry, yes, of course. Follow me back up to the house. Might there be some way of connecting the pool area to the garden?"

Dorus led the way and rooms switched their lighting off as they departed. Once outside, Dorus again berated himself about how badly he had designed things.

"Look, here is the garden. It is really not laid out well. There is plenty of room but I've never got around to sorting it out. Partly because of this – the archaeological bit." He let his eyes lower to look at the ground by their feet. "Until we can sort this out, I don't want to make any big decisions. You really can't see much - just a load of bushes – but there is something under there. It needs investigation and then it needs an Annie to work out how to make sense of the house, the underground emporium and the archaeology. It's a real mess. I hope you are going to perform a miracle for me."

"I'm definitely up for giving it a go. But I think I'm going to need a week just to come to terms with the cars, the bunker the pool and everything. Seriously, Dee, it's a hell of a lot to get my head around."

"Sorry. I absolutely promise there's nothing else. Cross my heart."

"Well, I think that's enough."

"Right. Back to the house. Let's just chill. Lunch is next and then let's think about dinner. You need to take a good look around and tell me what you need to buy in for when you become chief chef."

"I get the feeling your life revolves around food and wine."

"Yes. Guilty as charged. Problem?"

"Nope. Actually, I think I'm going to fit right in."

"Oh. Just one last thing. Just a small matter of the burden. I can tell you I'm up for passing the burden on to you. But are you up for accepting it?"

"I think you already know, Dee. I think I accepted the burden some while back. Probably whilst we were in Provence. Probably when we were watching the shooting stars and making wishes. We just didn't say it."

"Yes. I thought so. But we just had to agree it. So, we've done the roundtrip, but your journey officially starts here."

"It's been quite a journey already, but I think I'm ready to do it now."

"That makes me very happy, Annie."

Having retrieved what was left of the stash of charcuterie they had transported from Provence, both Dorus and Anaya fell headlong into nostalgic moods.

"Ruth would be very proud of me, wouldn't she, Dee? After a chance meeting at a party, I have wrenched the stick from up my backside and I have really taken her advice about going on a rollercoaster."

"I guess the trick is enjoying the ride."

"Indeed so, but also remembering not to stop. If I stopped to think, I reckon I'd be petrified. I've changed so much and so fast."

"Maybe don't stop, but at least slow down. Change is good, but it's also good to let yourself catch-up with yourself from time to time."

"Slow down to catch up, eh? Is that a new song or one you've already done?"

"You are sharp. Yes. One I already did. But stop fishing. You know I can't tell you which my songs are. It frustrates the hell out of me, actually. I really want to tell you."

"Don't worry. I get it. So, Dee, what's next today?"

"Just chill, I think. Maybe you could make me a shopping list of things you want for cooking. And how about booking up some driving lessons? That might be enough for today."

"Will do."

"Then maybe a swim before dinner and an early night."

"Perfect. Only thing is I didn't bring a swimming costume. I wasn't planning for an underground swimming pool."

Dorus returned a contemplative look before Anaya spoke the words he was thinking.

"Oh. Yes. Of course. Skinny dipping was on the list along with the *al fresco* showers, wasn't it? And the Jacuzzi and the sauna. If I didn't know better, I'd think this is all a plan to get me to take my kit off!"

"No! Oh my God, no!"

"Don't panic. Just kidding. I know you are not like that. Well, I'm still on my journey of discovery, so skinny dipping it is. If I had the bottle to do that *al fresco* shower with you, then skinny dipping won't feel half as bad. First things first though, let me take a look around your kitchen. I must say, it looks a dream to cook in. Maybe you could find me a driving school number to call. Let's strike whilst the iron is hot."

After sweeping around the kitchen, Anaya returned with a small list of spices and long list of compliments about the layout of the kitchen.

"You really made the kitchen the heart of the house, didn't you? I love it. I love the way the kitchen looks out over the living area which then carries your eyes over the dining space to the sea. It works really well. You definitely got some things right here, but yes, the whole site does need some careful thought to make all the bits work together. I bet there is a narrative to be told, but I'm still trying to read it."

"Thanks. The whole place is still a big muddle. But from what you are saying you've at least grasped the problem."

"Not going to lie, Dee, it is a disaster. Or, at least it is a lot of really good bits that, when put together, make a disaster. I've actually already had some thoughts though, but I'm not sharing yet. I think the missing link is the archaeology. Did you say the local archaeological group has already had a look?"

"Well, the university did. I think there's an amateur archaeological group which is very active. It might be worth contacting them."

"OK. I'll do some Googling. We really need to get a full geophysics survey to find out what's going on down there. Then we can piece the history of this place together which should inform the overall narrative of the design."

"You sound like an architect, Annie."

"Yup. Through and through. But this is fun. I'm genuinely looking forward to it. Depending what the geophysics shows there might need to be an excavation. Are you happy about them digging up your garden?"

"More than happy. In fact, I'd want to join in."

"Yeah. Me too."

They both tapped with determination on the keyboards of their respective laptops until Dorus found a local driving school with a female driving instructor curiously named Ermentrude and Anaya located and telephoned a local archaeological society who were incandescent with excitement about the prospect of being let loose on a new site which might conceal the remains of a mediaeval church.

Dorus drifted into light sleep on the sofa and Anaya drifted into the kitchen to prepare a simple dinner of onion bhajis and lamb saag using ingredients she had already located.

Dorus stirred again and Anaya presented him with both a mug of tea and with tantalising aromas from her culinary endeavours.

"Wow. What service. You're hired."

"Glad to please, sir. Dinner about six, OK? It'll look after itself in the oven until then."

"Wonderful. After I've woken up do you still fancy a swim?"

"Definitely."

Slowly, Dorus caught up with Anaya's enthusiasm and wakefulness.

"Right. There should be a robe in your bedroom. If you want to get changed up there, I'll meet you by the pool in ten."

"OK. In ten. Then, skinny dipping; another new experience for me. Because I haven't had enough new experiences since I met you."

"As long as they are good experiences that's all that matters."

"So far so good, Dee."

Ten minutes later Dorus reappeared from his bedroom and skipped down the stairs wearing a heavy, navy, towelling robe. Anaya, wearing a white robe was already in the kitchen stirring and checking pans. Downing her wooden spoons, she replaced saucepan lids and returned the pans to the large, stainless-steel ovens. She met Dorus' eyes and nodded.

Dorus led the way down the steep wooden steps into the cellar and onwards to the door of the pool area.

"Look. The switches are here. Just put all of them to 'on' and everything is ready to use."

Then, as he pushed the door open, Anaya saw the lights were on, relaxing mood music was playing and the pool cover was remotely rolling back to reveal the rippling aquamarine water.

"We just need to get the cover off the Jacuzzi. Maybe give me a hand. It's always switched on so it'll be good and warm. The sauna is on now but it takes about half an hour to come up to heat. So, if we have a swim and a Jacuzzi, then it will probably be about ready."

After removing the cover from the Jacuzzi and letting steam begin rising from its turquoise blue depths, Anaya removed her robe abruptly and discarded it over a poolside lounger whilst simultaneously turning away from Dorus in order to execute an impressive dive. Dorus had no time to offer her an opportunity to swim alone if skinny dipping made her feel uncomfortable. Dorus disrobed and followed her into the pool somewhat more cautiously and began what appeared to be a cross between doggy paddle and breast stroke whilst Anaya switched from front crawl to back crawl with intermittent bouts of powerful butterfly stroke. The water appeared to part before her in acceptance of her swimming mastery and then close again behind her creating an impressive wake.

As Dorus reached the conclusion of his first length, Anaya completed her third and pulled up next to him.

"Christ, Annie. Where did you learn to swim like that?"

"I used to leave the house in the morning before the rest of my housemates were up and there's a swimming pool on my way to work so I used to do half an hour or so there every morning. It really woke me up and kept me fit. It was all part of my mental diversion strategies. I told myself it would make me even better at work. Shame it didn't help me keep my job though."

"Well, you might not have kept your job, but you obviously have another career as a professional swimmer."

"Flattery! Keep it up, Dee. Anyway, you were right as usual. Skinny dipping is awesome. I have never felt so free – except perhaps showering *al fresco* in Provence."

"Yeah. You can come and use the pool any time. You know how to switch it all on. Just switch it off as you leave. Right, another couple of lengths for me and about another twenty for you, then I'm off to the Jacuzzi."

Dorus continued his pedestrian natation as Anaya lapped him with relentless repetitiveness.

Dorus first and then Anaya exited the pool and slid into the Jacuzzi and both took the soothing warmth and effervescence as an opportunity to relax and unwind from their travels and their emotional trials.

"I just don't get Jacuzzis, Annie."

"What do you mean?"

"It's basically a bowl of hot, fizzy water. I don't get why it is just so completely relaxing."

"And yet it so is. I love it. I've never had a sauna though. That's just a very hot room. Where's the fun in that?"

"Wait and see."

The sauna experience came next and now they sat properly aware for the first time of each other's nakedness in the intense heat as their bodies began beading with sweat.

"OK. I get it. Saunas are totally relaxing too. This could all become a bit of a habit, Dee."

"Most definitely. Plus, we've got a lot of sightseeing to do since you've not been to Cornwall before. I'll be your guide. Then you've got your driving lessons. Then you've got the archaeological dig to do. Then you've got to come up with the most amazing design in the world to make *Meneghiji* become whole."

"*Meneghiji?*"

"*Meneghiji*. It's what I call this place. It's Cornish for a sanctuary; a refuge; a safe place."

"Very apt."

"It's your safe place too now. For as long as you want to stay."

"Great. My plan is to totally overstay my welcome. It's just all too brilliant."

"It wouldn't be possible for you to overstay your welcome. Just treat it like home."

"Thanks. I'll make myself useful so you don't want to kick me out. You are right. I have got lots to keep me going. What about you? What are your plans?"

"As I say, I've got to get my head into the studio and start turning all the ideas I've been jotting down into actual songs. I have a client waiting. I'm still a bit worried, though. The songs are beginning to shape up more like actual love songs than songs of broken love and desperation. Maybe this is the end. Maybe I can't write anymore. I knew it would come to an end one day."

"I'm sure it will all start to come together once you get going. Maybe if I seriously piss you off, you'll do angry songs again."

"I'm not sure you could piss me off. Turns out you are easy to hang out with. Who would have thought?"

"You aren't so bad yourself, Mr. Dee. Changing the subject. I was thinking about the design. I need some history. Do you know why the MoD chose here to build the bunker?"

"Nope. The MoD won't give anything away, but there is a rumour that a giant transatlantic cable comes ashore somewhere near here. Apparently, it's a major communications link. Maybe that was important if the war cabinet needed to have good links. But I'm only guessing. I think there is a cable called the Apollo North Cable somewhere, but I've not the slightest idea where it is. Maybe nowhere near here but maybe right here under us."

"Interesting. Even if the cable isn't here, the rumour that it might be is enough to help me understand what's going on."

"I can't wait for the excavation to begin. Any idea when it might be."

"The guy I spoke to said it might be in a couple of weeks. Just a quick look first, then he'll come up with a plan. He said if there is some sort of church down there then he will need to report it to the Council for British Archaeology. Then put a team together. Then spend possibly many months excavating and logging it for posterity. So, we'll have to see."

"Exciting stuff. What about your dream building too? You must have a big design in your head that you'd love to build given half the chance."

"Not just in my head. It's my final design project from college. It needs loads more work, but what it really needs is a customer with really deep pockets. I went large. Think major concert hall in a major city. Trouble is, no one would even look at my design. They work with big companies with big reputations. That's why I was so excited getting the job I had. I thought they might give me the chance to lead a project to bring my design into reality after I proved myself to them. Shame it all came to nothing just because I wouldn't shag my boss. I'll show it to you after dinner."

"Keep dreaming. You never know. It could still happen. By the way, do you need equipment if you are going to do a design for this place?"

"Maybe. I can do most things on my laptop, but if it gets serious then maybe I'd need some more software. For big designs I'd do models and stuff too, but let's see how it goes for a bit. I'll let you know if I need anything. Is it OK if I spend time on my signature design too?"

"You seriously don't need to ask. Remember that this burden thing is all about you creating your own world. You are in charge."

"OK. I'll get used to it in time."

"You have time. You have all the time you need. All the time you want. That's really the only thing I can provide. Meanwhile, on a practical matter, I'll get a credit card sorted for you so you can buy whatever you need when you need it. I'll sort that out when we go back upstairs."

Dorus allowed his eyes to close and to allow the heat of the sauna to penetrate deep into his body. Anaya allowed herself to watch sweat trickle down his tight torso as it mirrored the contours of his musculature before flicking her eyes away to divert them to the thermometer mounted on the wall of the sauna.

"Right, Dee, I'm cooked. Quick shower and then I'll get dinner finished."

"I won't be long. You go ahead and I'll be up in fifteen minutes."

Anaya left the heat of the enclosed, red cedar box and stood under one of the two showers unaware that Dorus was able to admire the soft contours of her athletic body through the glass door of the sauna. Dorus did not divert his eyes.

The evening progressed with dinner, casual conversation, a visual tour of Anaya's dream project on her laptop and an early night.

*****

Two weeks passed whilst Dorus submerged himself in his song writing and Anaya progressed with her driving lessons. Whilst waiting for the initial visit from the archaeologists she had also spent time refining and developing her ideas for her 'signature design' which Dorus had nicknamed *Anaya's Folly*. They swam daily, they hiked the coastal paths and moors, they visited the Eden Project, Land's End, the Tate Modern in St Ives and The Lost Gardens of Heligan. Mostly, they talked. They talked about their pasts but little of their futures despite Anaya giving up her rented room in Islington and moving her official residency address to Dorus' Cornish cottage, *Meneghiji.* They reconciled this decision as a sensible and rational move albeit a temporary one until Anaya decided on her future path.

*****

A bright, refreshed morning bathed the stone cottage and welcomed Dorus and Anaya down to breakfast on what had planned to be a routine day of working on designs and songs but which changed rapidly as Dorus greeted Anaya with an invitation to lunch on the Isles of Scilly.

"What do you think Annie? Fancy a day off and a quick jaunt to the Scillies for lunch?"

"Sounds amazing. How does it work, then? Do we fly there? Do we go by boat?"

"Fly. But hang on to your croissant. We fly there in my plane."

"What do you mean? *In your plane.*"

"What I say. I have a little plane. It's a Piper Archer. Dead sweet. So, we can fly over there, have lunch and fly back."

"OK, Dee. I suppose I should be getting used to these things from you, but I'm not. In fact, I think I remember you had no more bomb shells to drop on me. So, you are a pilot and you own your own plane?"

"Sounds odd when you say that, but yes. It's only a little one. It's not as though I fly Jumbos, or anything. I got my Private Pilot Licence when some money started rolling in. It really occupied my mind. Really helped me get myself together. Flying a plane focuses the mind a bit. You can't be thinking about other things when you are landing a plane on a strip of tarmac. You kind of have to focus a bit. Getting it wrong isn't really an option."

"Good point."

"I had no intention of buying a plane but then more money rolled in and this Piper came up for sale. It was one of the flying school members at Newquay Flying School. He needed to get rid of it. It was a good price - too much to resist, so I bought it."

"Learning you are pilot and own you own plane is a big deal and yet you make it sound so, er, *normal*."

"Seriously no big deal. Sorry I didn't tell you before. It just didn't crop up. Anyway, it's a lovely day and I have to fly to keep my hours up to keep my licence current. So, what do you say?"

"Yes – obviously. When?"

"Just give me half an hour to plot a route and stuff and then we can head to Newquay Airport. It won't take me long. I know the route off by heart, but I still have to go through the rigmarole of plotting and planning. I just need to check the AIRMETS and make a few calculations."

"AIRMETS?"

"Meteorology. There's an aviation site. It gives the weather conditions at various heights above the ground. It's dead accurate. Really important in a light aircraft. Don't want to get caught out."

"Now you're scaring me. Say no more. Right. I'll get ready. Anything I need? A parachute or something."

"Very funny. No. Come as you are."

Dorus plotted a route and made phone calls to get permission to land at St Mary's Airport on the Isles of Scilly. A short drive to Newquay Airport in the *bug-eye* ended in a carpark reserved for general aviation pilots and Dorus donned a small buoyancy aid and a high visibility jacket and handed similar ones to Anaya. He checked in, signed paperwork and then they walked to a row of small light aircraft alongside a grey, metal hangar. After a visual inspection, Dorus climbed into the pilot's seat of his Piper with Anaya alongside him in the co-pilot's seat, both now wearing headsets.

"Right, Annie, this will seem a bit odd, but I'm bound by aviation law to do the whole safety speech thing just like on big planes, then we can be off. So, listen up. There is the yoke and pedals in front of you. Try not to grab them. In the event of an emergency release your harness and evacuate on my command but not before. Follow my instructions at all times. OK?"

"OK. So basically, just do what I'm told."

"Exactly. I am technically not just the pilot but I'm also in command. But most of all, just enjoy the flight. You can talk to me on the headset. You don't need to press buttons or anything, just speak normally. Now, I've got to finish the safety checks inside then off we go."

Dorus proceeded to talk to himself whilst checking controls and instruments before chatting to the control tower, starting the engine and then taxiing to a holding point where he performed final engine checks and awaited permission to take off.

Finally, Dorus taxied to the start of the runway, pushed the throttle fully open and the Piper roared and rattled forwards towards the sea until he pulled back on the yoke and smooth air lifted them to four thousand feet where he levelled out and banked steeply to the right to follow the Cornish coast northwards.

"Wow, Dee. It's so beautiful. But aren't the Scillies the other way?"

"They are indeed. But we are going joy riding. North for a while until we get to Bude, then we turn right and go cross country until we hit the south coast near Plymouth. Then we can track the coast all the way around to Lands End. Then off to St Marys."

"This is just too amazing, Dee! This has to be the best way of seeing Cornwall."

The flight proceeded and Dorus enthusiastically pointed out land marks in-between chattering to Air Traffic Control in an abbreviated language which was incomprehensible to Anaya.

"See over there, Annie. Can you see the clay pits and Eden?"

"Wow! Yes."

"Are you ready?

"What for?"

"Just do as I say. Right. Put your feet on the pedals in front of you. Now hold the yoke. OK. Now I'm releasing the controls to you. Just fly level and steady."

Dorus sat back, released his yoke and, in a comedic gesture, folded his arms to demonstrate that Anaya was now controlling the Piper.

"Oh, my God, Dee! Am I actually flying the plane?"

"You are! Are you OK?"

"A bit terrified!"

"They say piloting a plane is 99% boredom and 1% sheer terror. But don't worry, I'll take back control for the scary bit when we land. Just stay level and keep the blue sea on the left and the green fields on the right. Watch these two instruments and try to keep them in the centre."

Anaya gripped tighter than necessary to the yoke and Dorus made fine adjustments until they headed over the sea towards the airport on the island of St Mary's.

"Right, Anaya, release the controls. I'm going to get us ready to land."

Further chatter to Air Traffic Control took place and Dorus brought the Piper down onto the runway and taxied to a parking place alongside the control tower. Having checked in and paid the landing fee they spurned the waiting taxis and headed on foot along a track into the centre of Hugh Town past the house once owned by Harold Wilson, the ex-Prime Minister of Great Britain who had named it *Lowenva* – Cornish for 'happy house'. A picnic lunch on the beach was enhanced by Dorus buying and presenting Anaya with a bucket and spade with which she constructed an impressive multi-turreted castle. Finally, they headed back to the airport after Dorus bought Anaya a gift of a sweatshirt emblazoned with '*IoS*'. A visit to the control tower and the completion of yet more paperwork prefaced the return flight to Newquay.

Instead of heading on a direct course back to the mainland, Dorus was granted permission to turn right after take-off and to execute a low-level flight around the islands before climbing to cruising height and speed and resuming the planned navigation. Sailors acknowledged them with waves of their hands and pods of dolphins and hump back whales played under their low-level flight trajectory.

Finally, they climbed to four thousand feet and bid farewell to their island adventure. The Cornish coast quicky came into view and Dorus tracked it back to Newquay. As the airport appeared in front of them, Dorus again chatted on the radio and corrected their approach for the runway designated by the air traffic controller.

"Right Annie. Just got to land and we are done. They say any landing that you can walk away from is a good landing, but an excellent landing is one you can walk away from *and* use the plane again."

"I'll be happy with either, Dee."

An excellent landing was completed, the Piper was parked and the inevitable paperwork was completed before they headed back to what now felt to be *their* home.

Over dinner they relived their day.

"Dee, that was amazing today. I'm just lost for words."

"Pretty cool, eh?"

"Do you fly to London and to France?"

"Can't fly to City Airport in London. The Piper is a single engine plane and it's against the law to fly over built-up areas where you can't glide away from houses to safety. I guess I could fly into Heathrow, but my little Piper would be like a fly on the windscreen of a Jumbo. Bit too scary for me. I'm just a hobby pilot. I suppose I could fly to France, but the nearest airfield is so far away from the cottage it's not really worth it."

"But can we fly around Britain?"

"Yes, of course. We'll have another trip some time."

"And can I take the controls again? It was a real adrenaline rush."

"Of course. Actually, it's not so hard flying a plane. You need a bit of courage to take off, but then you just sit back and enjoy the scenery. The real trick is knowing where and how to land. That's both the best bit and the scary bit."

"Oh, Dee. Very clever. I see what you did there. That was a metaphor for the burden giving thing, wasn't it? I had the courage to take off so now I'm to enjoy the flight but sooner or later I've got to have the bottle to decide where to land and then do an excellent landing. Very clever."

"I thought you might spot that. Actually, Annie by the sounds of it you're going to want to get a pilot's licence once you've learned to drive a car."

"One thing at a time, Dee."

The evening rolled into night and the days rolled into one another as they established what became a routine of architectural designing, song writing and swimming interrupted by walking and sightseeing. Anaya's driving lessons progressed smoothly and they spent many hours bonding in a shared enthusiasm for cooking and dining.

*****

Both Dorus and Anaya were impatient for the start of the archaeological survey which they had rightly concluded held the final bit of the jigsaw and which was needed to begin the design and reconstruction of *Meneghiji*. When a phone call confirmed the imminent arrival of a team of archaeologists who were to undertake an initial geophysics survey their excitement was hard to conceal. The archaeology group finally arrived at the agreed time and Anaya greeted them at the gate and directed them up the drive towards the house where, after a quick visual inspection, they retrieved their geophysics equipment from the rear of their Land Rover and began their meticulous and precise survey of the terrain surrounding the cottage.

Convening with both Dorus and Anaya later that afternoon, they presented their preliminary findings.

"Well, there is definitely a structure down there. It's impossible to be sure without excavating, but so far what we think is that it is *not* a chapel. Nothing in the layout suggests

211

anything other than a farm building dating back maybe about three hundred years or so. Sorry if that is a disappointment."

Anaya took charge of the conversation and Dorus listened in.

"No, not at all. We had no expectations. We just wanted to get an understanding of the site."

"Well, there is something interesting though. You see, your cottage, just as you thought, has been built out of the stone from the original building. We're fairly sure of that because there is evidence of the stone near the surface which we quickly uncovered. It looks like the same stone your house is made of. It is not unusual for stone from a farm building to be recycled like this. Again, only a full excavation would confirm it, though."

"OK. Interesting. Good to know."

"But here's the most interesting thing. We don't think your cottage was actually ever built as a cottage."

Dorus and Anaya leaned in to focus as he continued.

"We also found evidence of some fairly heavy-duty cables running from the bunker to what is now your cottage. We've come across this before. There's something similar up at Rame. What we found there was what looks like an old stone chapel but what is, in fact, an old-World War Two radar station."

Dorus and Anaya exhaled, raised their eyebrows and lifted their heads to denote their fascination.

"Yes. Everything we are seeing here is the same pattern. So, if we are right, an old stone barn was robbed to build a radar station which then fed directly into the underground bunker. The fact the radar station looked like a house was simple deception. The Luftwaffe flying overhead would not have any idea that a radar station and command bunker were hidden down here so they would just fly on to bomb the navy port at Plymouth. Which they did – a lot. They totally flattened Plymouth. It all ties in perfectly. I'll write to the MoD to see if they will confirm it, but they'll deny all knowledge of it most likely. The only way to be absolutely sure would be to excavate."

"Wow. That really is genuinely interesting. Where is all the radar equipment then?"

"Oh, that would have been stripped out after the war. The MoD is a bit fussy about leaving high tech equipment lying around for anyone to come along and nick. Especially the enemy."

"So, this whole site is basically a World War Two radar station and spare command bunker."

"Well, originally a farm building, then a World War two site. Whether or not it was ever used is another matter. We believe there are several sites like this around the country which were never used. All just constructed in case they were needed."

"Wow! Thanks. That's just fantastic. What's next?"

"Well, I will have to report my findings to the powers that be but I think they will just log it and not declare it needing protecting or anything. The most interesting bit of this site is your cottage and its bunker, not the old stone barn which has already been robbed out. In an ideal world I would like to run a couple of trenches across the site to confirm all this but I have to honest, it will really mess up your garden. And it'll be expensive. There's no way of avoiding it. We'd do our best to be tidy but frankly we'll leave a lot of bare soil needing landscaping after we've gone. What do you think?"

Dorus interjected.

"Most definitely. Yes p*lease.* Just dig up as much as you like. We're going to develop the site anyway so make as much mess as you want. When can you start?"

"Great. Well, we are just finishing off at a site on Bodmin Moor, so I could probably put a team together and get cracking in a couple of weeks. Assuming it confirms what I've just told you and we don't dig up anything earth shattering it will probably take us maybe a month to complete and then we can leave you in peace."

"Perfect. What do you think, Annie? Are you happy with that?"

"Very happy." Then, returning the conversation to the head of the archaeologic survey team. "And can I be a volunteer. I would love to get my hands dirty. I'm actually an architect and I'm going to try to design a new build here to reflect the history of the site."

"You most certainly can. Look, I'll write all this up and I'll have to give you some idea of the cost. This doesn't come cheap I'm afraid. We use volunteers as far as we can, but it has to be done properly which means carefully which means it is very labour intensive. Plus, there's the hire of diggers and stuff."

"No problem." Reassured Dorus. "If it's OK, deal directly with Anaya. She'll be your point of contact. OK, Annie?"

"Yes, indeed."

Following the visit, life resumed its routine. Dorus increasingly spent days in his studio emerging from time to time looking stressed and worried. Anaya continued designing both her signature building, *Anaya's Folly*, but now also she advanced her ideas for the Cornish site. She continued her driving lessons and successfully completed the theory test prior to an upcoming practical test. For both of them life was busy and fulfilling.

The excavation got underway and was eventually completed without any new discoveries. Anaya immersed herself in the dig, in her driving lessons and in her two architectural projects. Whilst Dorus immersed himself in his song writing.

One afternoon, Dorus emerged from his studio late in the afternoon after a marathon session, unshaven and gaunt.

"Well, Annie, it's done."

"The album? Congratulations. Shouldn't you be celebrating? You look like you've just been run over by a bus."

"We'll see. I've sent it off. But I reckon I'm finished. These songs are just so different. I don't think he'll want them. This might be the end of the road for my song writing."

"Don't be such a misery. He may love them."

"Maybe. I'm going for a stroll. I need to clear my head. Then maybe I'll have a swim. Are you on top of dinner, or shall I do something?"

"You go and get some fresh air and I'll prep dinner and then maybe I'll join you for a swim too."

Dorus headed to the clifftop to drink in the salt air and let the sea massage his angst whilst Anaya busied herself preparing Chicken Karahi which she had perfected having been let loose in Dorus' kitchen.

Dorus returned looking no better. They went skinny dipping together, they rested in the Jacuzzi and they soaked in the heat of the sauna but Dorus remained tense and uncommunicative. Even the aroma and subtlety of the Chicken Karahi didn't draw him out until, as they sat with a glass of wine looking out over a restless sea with their appetites satiated, Anaya snapped.

"For Christ's sake, Dee. Spit it out. You are seriously head doing. Just say it. Whatever it is."

"I'm sorry. It's just. Er, whilst I was out walking, he called me."

"Who?"

"My client – Jesus, I wish I could say his name."

"And? Didn't he like your stuff then?"

"He loved it. He wants to buy it. He wants to meet up at Faulty Towers in a couple of weeks to sing through it with me."

"What am I missing here? That's all brilliant news. How come you are in such a grump?"

"It's what he said."

"Bloody hell, Dee. Put me out of my misery. What is it?"

Dorus sighed and threw his head back to stare at the ceiling in order to avoid making eye contact with his inquisitor.

"He said that he loved the songs. He said an album of love songs is just what his fans want right now. It fits in perfectly with his life - he has just got married so love songs work well for him."

"Still not getting this, Dee. It all sounds perfect. Go on."

"He said that did I know I had written the songs for you. I told him not to be ridiculous and I told him there was no way that I had written them about you. He said no, not *about* you, *for* you."

"Oh! Shit. And ...."

"What if he is right? What if I just wrote a whole load of love songs for you?"

The length of the pause that followed the rhetorical nature of the question strained like a dam about to burst. Anaya had to push through the impasse and spoke in slow, quiet, reassuring tones.

"Well, Dee. Did you?"

217

"I just don't know. If I did then what does it mean?"

Anaya again allowed a pause to be sure that she had the courage to form an answer.

"That you love me?"

"Fuck! That can't be. Pandora's box would have dragged me in and eaten me alive. It can't be."

"Right. Cards on the table time, Dee. I actually have a theory about it. Brace yourself." She fixed her eyes resolutely as though about to give a reprimand. "Just maybe you've spent years writing songs feeding off the contents of your Pandora's box. Just maybe you emptied it and didn't realise it. Just maybe you have ended up being scared of an empty box."

"Christ, Annie. Are you planning a new career as a shrink?"

"That's it. I just peaked on the shrink front. I think I'll stick to designing buildings. Much safer."

The air between them stagnated whilst Anaya waited for a response that didn't come until she finally continued.

"Dorus, do you remember the mad soothsayer on the boat in Cannes?"

"Yes, of course. How could I forget?"

"She said that you needed to look into your box and that I was the key. Well ….."

"So, what are you saying? That I've ballsed everything up and gone and fallen in love with you?"

"Why ballsed it up?"

"Well, messed up our relationship. Our safety zone. You know. It was all working. Just as friends. Now, I'm about to screw it all up with a one-sided love affair."

"Hum. Brace yourself again, Dee."

"What now?"

"Well, it may not be just one sided?"

"What?"

"Yeah, you see, I might just have fallen in love with you a bit too."

"This can't be happening. When? When did you fall in love with me?"

"Well, I had a bit of a moment in Provence. You know when we were making wishes under the shooting stars?"

"Yes, of course."

"Well, that was a bit of a moment, but I buried my feelings pretty fast. But, but ...."

"Then what, Annie? Go on. You may as well say it now."

"Well, do you remember after we showered together when we'd finished chopping wood?"

"Of course I remember."

"Well, er – that's when I really felt it. When we were standing totally naked together looking out across the valley. It was the most beautiful thing I could imagine. Everything just seemed to slot into place. For those few minutes I just felt that I loved you."

"What? Really?"

"Afraid so, Dee. Sorry."

"Did you not think that you might mention it?"

"No. Absolutely not. If you remember, we very quickly established a safety zone when we first met. A safety zone which, by the way, has been pretty robust up until now. So, I just hid my feelings - from myself. I'm really good at that. Friendship did me just fine. But then ….."

"Go on, Annie. No stopping now."

"Well, that night on the boat when we crossed the channel in the storm and you hugged me to calm me down. I, er, might just have given in to my feelings at that point."

"My God! I just don't know what to do with all this."

"Well, for a start, you can stop freaking out. Your voice is getting worryingly high. Look. Nothing has changed. Just substitute 'love' for 'friendship' and we are still OK."

"In a parallel world maybe. Christ. I'm going to need some time."

"Dee. I'm really loving living here. I'm loving living here with you. I'm loving working on the designs for you. I don't want anything to change. Or, if it does change then just let it change for the better. We can still be friends. Just much closer friends."

"Well, I'm not throwing you out so let's just go ahead and see if I can stop panicking."

"Come here you."

Anaya slid across the sofa and cuddled up to Dorus who reciprocated and eventually relaxed into what was a genuine embrace. Anaya looked up into his eyes and they kissed a light but almost electric kiss followed by a smile whilst their hearts pounded against each other's ribs.

back to London

The moment of realisation which had brought their hearts and their souls together kept both Dorus and Anaya awake that night. The weather had deteriorated and rain drummed the windows and wind rattled the slate roof. In the early hours, a lull in the weather brought no further prospect of sleep and Dorus slipped into his dressing gown and crept to the kitchen to seek solace in a cup of tea. As he descended the stairs, he became aware of a dim light illuminating the kitchen where he found Anaya already filling a kettle.

"Oh, sorry Dee. Did I wake you?" she whispered.

"No. Not at all. I haven't slept yet. Are you brewing a cup?"

"Yup. Do you want one?"

"Please."

Anaya arranged two mugs and the kettle began to crackle and wheeze.

"Well, Dee. You chose a good time to induce insomnia by telling me you love me."

"What do you mean? I can't think of any good time."

"Don't you remember what day it is tomorrow? Er, I mean today."

"Oh, shit. Yes. I'm being self-absorbed again, aren't I? It's your driving test."

"Yes, it bloody well is and I'm probably going to fall asleep at the wheel now. Couldn't you have just waited another day before dropping the 'love bomb' on me?"

"Sorry about that, Annie. Actually, wasn't it you that told me that I love you?"

"Don't split hairs. I've decided to blame you for me failing my test."

"Fair enough."

Anaya completed the tea making and handed a steaming mug to Dorus. They both sat on the sofa and cradled their mugs with both hands looking down at the floor pensively.

"Thanks, Annie. Just a thought. How about taking these to bed whilst we sit the storm out and decide what to do with our lives?"

Whether intended or not, Anaya nodded and followed Dorus to his room where they climbed into his bed still robed. The lull in the storm began yielding to more rain and rumbles of thunder and their resolve to talk gave way to contemplative silence.

The tea, once drunk, coincided with increasingly frequent lightning flashes and more aggressive thunder. They both continued grasping their now empty mugs but remained silent until the strength of the storm overwhelmed Anaya.

"OK. That's a full-on thunder storm now, Dee. Not my favourite type of weather. You are going to have to look after me again until it goes. This is a bit of a *déjà vu*. A bit like the channel crossing. I think I could do with another hug."

"Don't worry. There are lightening conductors everywhere. We'll be safe."

"Yes, I know, I'm an architect remember. I know how lightening conductors work. But that's not the point."

The thunder and lightning aligned and synchronised as the storm took residence overhead and Dorus offered an all-embracing hug which Anaya accepted without reservation.

"Christ, Annie, you are shaking."

"Shut up and hold me."

Lying beneath an electrical storm in a tight embrace began to clear the stormy emotions that had been keeping sleep from them. The night sky eventually began to resume some degree of calm as the storm decided it had completed its task. Their misgivings followed the storm's lead and found some degree of stillness. Even when the thunder had become no more than a distant echo, they held each other as though making up for lost opportunities.

"Dorus."

"That sounds serious. You never call me Dorus."

"Dorus. Don't read too much into this, but can we take our dressing gowns off? It's really uncomfortable and, I don't know, I just want to be as close as I can with you right now. Sorry, is that too weird? It's just ..... I just really want to be close to you. I feel in such a muddle."

224

Dorus offered no verbal response but slipped his dressing gown off and waited for Anaya to reciprocate his lead. Now both naked, they lay as one in silence as their souls followed the lead of their bodies and found convergence. Occasional lightening from across the sea interrupted the darkness and momentarily illuminated their lives. Still devoid of sleep Anaya rolled on top of Dorus, sat up straddling his groin and whispered almost imperceptibly.

"Can I feel you, Dee? It's time for me to face my demons."

"Yes, of course."

Anaya reached down between her legs and her hand encircled Dorus' penis cautiously. She found an immediate response and then with some degree of hesitation she lifted herself up and then lowered herself again onto him allowing his erection to slide inside her. She became motionless and statuesque as she slowly accepted that her life had just undertaken a quantum leap. Dorus lay motionless as his breathing deepened until he pushed himself up on his arms to allow his lips to meet hers in a gossamer soft, lingering kiss. In response, Anaya wrapped her legs around him and they established a perfect physical and emotional balance.

"Wow, Dee, I'm not even panicking." Anaya whispered into Dorus' ear allowing her breath to create tingles in his body.

"Nor me."

"Can we just stay like this forever."

"Until we die. Then maybe one day an archaeologist will dig up our bones all mingled together."

"They'll probably conclude we died in mortal combat."

"Shut up and kiss me."

Brief kisses paved the way for long, lingering kisses. And, as memories of the storm's climax dissipated, they reached theirs without the need for exertion after which they lay together, their limbs intertwined, slumped in a deep, post-orgasmic sleep.

The light of the morning eventually penetrated their shared consciousness and brought them to a hazy and confusing awakening. Rather than immediately face the cataclysmic theatre of the previous night, Dorus fetched more tea.

"Well, Dee. I don't know what to say."

"Then don't. There's no need."

"No going back now."

"Nope. No going back. So, let's go forwards – together."

"Happily, Dee. Happily. But first things, first. I've got a bloody driving test in about two hours! I realise something big just happened, but I have to focus on my test. I promise to be more romantic once it's out the way. Sorry."

"No being sorry, Annie, we'd better get going. Now, are you ready for one more hurdle?"

"What now?"

"Follow me."

Dorus slipped from beneath the duvet and led the way to the en-suite bathroom.

"Remember I told you about the *his and hers* handbasins? I said you'd probably never actually see them. How wrong was I?"

Anaya accepted the prompt and turned taps to summon hot water in the double shower as Dorus quickly dragged a razor over his stubble before joining her. Washing themselves and each other felt like washing the tragedies of their past out of their lives and celebrating the happiness of their new lives. Breakfast followed but was left uneaten and Anaya waited for her driving instructor to arrive for a final drive culminating in her test. After her departure, Dorus entered his studio and wrote one more love song – this time, he wrote it knowingly *for* Anaya.

*****

Judging that Anaya would be returning soon, Dorus made his way back up the wooden steps in the cellar into the living room to be faced with the sight of her, already having arrived back, slouched on the sofa weeping breathlessly. Dorus spoke in whispered tones to her.

"Oh, Annie, I'm so sorry. Don't worry. No-one passes first time."

Dorus' voice exacerbated her distress and her sobs became uncontrollable as she launched herself at him, wrapped her arms around his body and buried her head in his chest.

"Oh, Dee. It was terrible."

"Don't worry."

"Dee. You love me ….. I love you ….. we made love ….. and now I get to drive the bug-eye and the Aston."

"What? You passed? You mean you passed? Why are you crying?"

"Because of everything! I've never been so happy. It's like years of pain I've been lugging around have just been lanced like a boil."

"Oh. So, being in love with me is like lancing a boil?"

"Exactly."

"Right. Well. Congratulations."

Anaya finally peeled herself off Dorus and began to control her breathing.

"Here, Annie. I've got a present for you."

He handed her an external hard drive and smiled.

"What? I was expecting flowers or chocolates or something. What's that?"

"The songs. Whilst you were out, I called my client. I told him that he was right. I wrote them *for* you. So here they are.

They are yours. I wrote an extra one whilst you were out. I called it *Annie's Burden*."

"What do you mean?"

"From me to you – with love. *Your* songs. The songs I wrote for *you*."

"Really?"

"Yes. What's more, I told him that if he wants to buy them, he'll have to buy them off you. They are yours to sell. They aren't mine now."

"But, it's all your work!"

"All written for you. It's my gift to you."

"Plus, I get to drive the bug-eye and the Aston?" Anaya's tears dried and her face lit up with relief. "Oh, Dee. I love you."

Their eyes fixed each other's and Dorus spoke in level monotones.

"I love you too."

The air between their eyes stood still until Dorus brought them back to pressing, practical matters.

"Now, we are due in London to meet the client in two weeks. We are to get there a couple of days early to meet with his solicitors. You are going to have to sign an NDA so that we can meet him together. His wife will be there too."

"Wow. This is all too good to be true."

"You know what they say. If it is too good to be true then it probably is ... well ..... here comes the bad news. I sort of offered that we'd cook them dinner for after he and I have finished singing through it all. Sorry."

"No problem. Sounds really cool."

"Except, when I say *we* will cook dinner I actually mean *you* will cook dinner – I'll be busy. I'm sorry. It just sort of slipped out."

"Dorus you dunderhead! No problem. Honestly. Just let me loose in that deluxe kitchen at Faulty Towers and I'll rustle up a banquet."

"Are you sure? Am I forgiven?"

"Forgiven, Dee."

"Right. Coffee and then you know what."

"What?"

"We are off for a drive in the bug-eye."

"Really?"

"It's important you get behind the wheel as soon as possible. What's more, let's take the Aston when we go to London and then do a quick trip to Provence in her. Share the driving this time."

"You are on, Dee! In the meantime, I'm going to put the finishing touches to the design for this place. Then it's show time!"

Dorus fiddled with the stereo system drawing from it the weaving, polyphonic tones of Robert Carver, a Scottish Renaissance composer, sung by Sir Harry Christopher's 'The Sixteen'.

"Perfect choice, Dee. Very relaxing. Just what I need. I'm going to sit here and finish my first attempt at the design for this place and then I'm going to do some more to my signature design. I have adopted a deconstructed Renaissance design for that so your choice of music is perfect. Then, after that, maybe I'll let you take me out for a spin at the wheel of the bug-eye. I just need to calm down a bit first. I'm feeling all over the place."

"All good with me. You know, we really are going to have to do it aren't we?"

"Yes, I promise. I just need to get myself together and then we'll take the bug-eye out."

"No, I mean the trip?"

"Provence?"

"Well, yes, but I meant the big trip. We need to visit the key architectural wonders you told me about. The ones that changed the world. You can soak in all the architecture and I can soak in all the music associated with it. Inspiration for both of us."

"Oh, Dee, are you serious?"

"Totally. It'll be, *Annie and Dee's Inspiration Tour.* You give me a list of buildings and I'll put an itinerary together. But first things first. You've got to get behind the wheel today and then we've got to do the London trip – oh, and Provence."

"On it!"

Anaya spent the next few hours putting the final touches to the design for *Meneghiji* and then announced she was ready to reveal it. Dorus joined her and she swivelled the screen of her laptop to angle the display towards Dorus.

"Christ, Dee. I'm as nervous as when I did my driving test."

"Don't be. I already love it."

"You've got to be honest. If you don't like it you've got to tell me. It just feels I've already travelled a long way to get to this point and, well, it's kind of personal."

"Relax. Talk me through it."

Anaya flicked through slide after slide enthusiastically describing details and design features.

"OK, so, Dee, I wanted to reflect what you had already done but then superimpose what we have unearthed. So, for a start, I propose a second skin around your original house because at the moment it is a single stone wall. Putting another skin around it will effectively make a cavity wall and we can put tons of insulation in the space. The inside dimensions of the house stay the same, but it gets a little bigger on the outside and that makes it more imposing. It also allows me to line up the outer walls of the house with the walls of the historic barn buried in the garden too. It also just gives enough extra space for me to create two sweeping ramps; one on either side of the house. One will give access to the bunker, the other to the suntrap outside the pool. I suggest you keep the entrance to the bunker you already have, although you won't need it anymore – just for historical honesty. Also, I know you have kept loads of bare concrete down in the bunker except for all that acoustic cladding in your studio, but I think it could be smartened up just by polishing it. It's not a big job, but it will make a big difference. Now, the new bit. Using the lines of the outer wall of the house we build a quadrangle over the lines of the archaeology. Around three sides we put various rooms, but in the middle, we put a walkway and raised flower beds. But look - here's the really interesting bit. Look at the roof over the quadrangle. There's a rectangular hole in the centre. So, rain will fall vertically down into the centre of the quad and fall into a water feature. It doesn't matter what direction the rain comes; it will always fall vertically into the quad. I actually nicked that idea from the Getty Villa in Los Angeles but I think it originates from ancient Rome. Anyway, the thing is, the archaeology is an old barn so inside the quad you could grow herbs and vegetables - to reflect the farming heritage. It'll also mean you can be a bit more self-sufficient. I was thinking of Sacha and Raphaël when I came up with that. Meanwhile, the outer skin of your house looks like a nineteenth century farmhouse and hidden in it are two easy access points to the bunker and the suntrap. So, it's a timeline from medieval farming to nineteenth century farmhouse to twentieth century World War Two artifact. Solar panels on the quad roof and a ground source heat pump system to harness natural heat from underground and

233

then you are just about off grid like your cottage in Provence."

Having paused long enough to allow Dorus a response, she looked up nervously at him.

"Well?"

Dorus' response was to pull her into his arms and kiss her.

"Annie, at the risk of inducing vomiting, I think you have transformed my house into our home. It's brilliant. It's incredible. You are a genius."

Anaya's response was to begin crying again and Dorus squeezed her tighter than was necessary.

"I just love it. I just love it, Annie. So, what happens next?"

After some minutes, Annie composed herself enough to find a reply.

"Oh, my God. I was so nervous. I really didn't know if you'd like it. My God, Dee, the last twenty-four hours have really drained me. Oh, there is one more thing. You don't have to agree, but you know the gym - the one neither of us ever use? Well, what if we keep it but halved it in size. Maybe I could make myself a little studio in there."

"You didn't need to worry, Annie. You've totally understood it. Better still, you've totally understood me. Everything has come together. And yes to the studio - his and hers studios opposite each other in the bunker. I love the idea. Tell me what you need in there and I'll get onto it. You've got your hands full."

"Phew. This has turned out to be a big twenty-four hours. So, anyway, I still have a lot to do. I have to change the design into detailed construction plans ready to submit for planning. Plus, you'll need landscapers for outside and inside the quad. That's above my paygrade I'm afraid. I'll get onto the planning application if you are sure."

"Totally sure, but after a drive!"

"Really, do I have to?"

"Yup. You get yourself together - I'll bring the *bug eye* up."

Together, but with Anaya in the driving seat, they drove the classic sports car through the Cornish lanes to St Agnes Beacon where they sat surveying both the ocean and their lives before returning for a swim, a sauna, dinner, an early night and to gentle love making before Anaya allowed her exhaustion to pave the way to a deep sleep followed eventually by Dorus.

*****

The next week was occupied by Anaya completing the planning application ready to submit to Cornwall Council for approval and by Dorus converting the gym into an architectural studio for Anaya. Together they planned and booked the *Annie and Dorus' Inspiration Tour*.

"Annie, I was thinking. You know when we are in London. Do you think we should invite Ruth and Derek around?"

"Oh, my God, yes. She'd kill us if we didn't see her."

"What does she know about *us*? Have you said anything to her? I haven't."

"Not much. I think I just told her that everything was going well and that you and me were getting on OK. I'll message her and invite them around. I'll just tell her we have some news. When is a good time?"

"Well, we arrive on Thursday and we've got a solicitor meeting on Friday morning for you to sign the NDA. He's coming to Faulty Towers. Then we've got the client meet on Saturday with dinner in the evening. So, see if they can do some time on Friday afternoon or evening. If not, then any time the following week. As always, we'll leave booking the Eurotunnel until the last minute so we can work around her diary. Then, when we are done, we'll head off to Provence."

"Right. I'll message her now. You know, last time you booked the Eurotunnel I was scared stiff. Now, well, I just plain can't wait. I can't wait to sit on *le trône* and to warm my toes by *la bête*. Maybe you'll trust me to do some cooking there this time."

"Me too. Actually, I was more nervous than I let on last time. But I reckon things might just have worked out OK."

"You reckon?"

Dorus poked her in the ribs.

*****

Ruth confirmed that she would visit them at Faulty Towers after she had finished at her Chambers and before she headed out with friends for a celebration. She would be alone as Derek was not around.

They packed for their road trip and eventually set off in the Aston Martin. Dorus powered up to the Taunton Deane service station on the M5 before handing over to Anaya who drove with extreme caution, mostly hugging the space behind slow, large lorries, onwards around the M4-M5 intersection before finally handing back to Dorus at the Leigh Delamere services for him to complete the final leg of the journey through the London traffic.

Arriving at Faulty Towers tired and relieved, Dorus routinely placed his hand on the biometric pads, firstly to open the garage doors and again to open the elevator doors. Stepping out into the penthouse felt like revisiting their past but in another dimension. They stood in front of the panoramic windows surveying their recent history which had come full circle but ended up in a different place.

A reheated lasagne which they had brought with them and a bottle of Valpolicella smothered them in satisfaction and warmth.

"Annie. I was thinking whilst you were driving."

"Uh oh, that usually means you are about to hit me with something."

"Well. I was thinking about your signature building, *Anaya's Folly.* How much would it take to build it?"

"How much would it cost; you mean?"

"Yeah."

"Impossible to say. It depends where for a start. Land prices vary enormously. Then there is the size. My design is scalable, so anything from a small project to a giant concert hall. Why? You got some loose change?"

"Well, you know I hate Faulty Towers. What if we sell it? Would that buy *Anaya's Folly*?"

"Sell it? What do you mean *sell it*? You mean you *own* it!?"

"Yes. Of course I do. You know I do. I told you that when we first met. In the summer house at Ruth's. You've always known."

"Er, no you didn't tell me. You said you had a place in Cornwall and a place in Provence and that you were staying in a penthouse where you met clients. You didn't say it was *your* penthouse. I've always assumed it was owned by a record company or something."

"Oops! No deception intended. I can see how that might have been a bit confusing."

"Holy crap! This place must be worth a fortune. I know a two-story penthouse went the other day for about two hundred million. Admittedly that was in Knightsbridge, but still, this is St Katharine Docks. It must be worth a fortune!"

"I guess so. As you know, when it was built it was just a shell. I invested in the penthouse and did it up like you see it now. I bought it for about five mill. Then gentrification happened. Then celebrities started moving here. Then the penthouse was suddenly the must-have pad for them. The value just skyrocketed."

"You are actually a bit of a money magnet, aren't you, Dee?"

"Hardly. But what do you think? Shall we sell up? Would it fund your new build somewhere?"

"It just may do. But do you seriously want to sell?"

"I seriously don't like it – and yes, I'd seriously sell. Tell you what. Let me give the agent I bought it through a call and we'll get a valuation. We can take it from there."

"OK. There's no harm investigating, I guess."

"Right. I'll give them a call right now."

*****

As Friday arrived, so did both the solicitor and the estate agent. Anaya half listened to the solicitor and Dorus followed the estate agent around the penthouse like a nodding dog.

When both the solicitor and the agent departed, Anaya and Dorus stood, face-to-face, looking at each other. Anaya broke the Mexican standoff.

"Who's going first ..... damn it! I'm going first. Dorus, you absolute nob-head. Sara Swati! Your client is Sara Swati? You .... you kept calling 'her' a 'he'. You know I'm a fan!"

"Sorry. I was really worried you might guess. Especially when you put her music on in the car. Christ, that drive was painful. You made me listen to an entire album of my own crap and I couldn't tell you."

"Dorus! I don't know what to say! You mean she is coming here tomorrow – and I'm cooking for her? Shit! She's a superstar – and I'm cooking for her!"

"Yes, and her husband. But don't worry. They are really nice. Not at all like their public image. And you can't tell anyone – you know that, right?"

"Yes, I know. The solicitor just spent the last hour telling me that in a hundred different ways. God, why are solicitors so boring. He didn't need to tell me the same thing a gazillion times."

"It's such a relief you know who it is now. I just can't tell you how much I've wanted to say her name to you. There were so many times that I nearly did. So, anyway, my news now. The agent says it is always hard to value something like this but he expects a lot of interest from a lot of very wealthy people. He said he has been showing an Arab oil sheik around various properties – or rather the sheik's agent. Apparently, he wants so buy a place for his daughter who starts university in London soon. He said he'd call him and see if there is interest. He said he'd start teasing potential clients too to start building some sort of bidding war. So, I told him to go ahead. I told him to go ahead but I didn't sign. I said I'd talk it over with you first because, if we sell, it means you go ahead with *Anaya's Folly*. That's a big decision for you."

"OK. Talk over. Just sign on the dotted line, Dorus."

"Seriously? Are you sure?"

"Sure."

"OK. I'll give him a call."

"So, I'd better think up a really special meal for tomorrow then."

"No, not at all. They are really down to earth. It'll be very casual."

"I'll take your word for it. Still, I'm off shopping to get stuff to cook. I'm cooking for Sara Swati, for Christ's sake! I'll pick up some cake too before Ruth gets here."

Once shopping was completed and Anaya had returned and organised herself in the kitchen, they waited for Ruth to arrive. As always, she arrived on time in a whirlwind of energy and excessive salutations.

"Darlings. So wonderful to see you both. Tell me all about it. I don't have long. Big celebration tonight. So, tell me everything."

"What's the celebration?"

"Oh, nothing much. Just my divorce came through today. Oh, don't say anything. You must have seen it coming. Everyone else did, apparently. Anyway, do you remember at my party when I interrupted you two love birds getting it together in the summerhouse? I was looking for Derek. Well, I found him in the attic room with Patricia-The-She-Whore riding his cock. I threw them out. Never let him back in. It spoiled the party a bit, I must say. Most people just left, but the ones I actually wanted to leave just stayed to comfort me. Anyway, I get to keep the house and everything since he didn't contribute a damn thing. He gets to keep Patricia-The-She-Whore though but unfortunately for him she doesn't want him now he doesn't have any of my money. I've no idea where he is. Probably couch surfing and shagging his latest little bitch. But at least he's not doing it at my expense any more. So, what's the news with you then?"

The pause, when it came, allowed Dorus and Anaya to offer their surprise and sadness at the news but Ruth discarded both sentiments with a wave of her hand and instead demanded that they update her on their news.

Dorus drew breath and exhaled his words.

"Well, Ruth, I guess the big news is that Anaya and I are – well, a couple."

"Yes! I know! I'm not stupid. I saw that coming a mile off. And no, before you ask, I didn't set you up at the party. It never crossed my mind. Well, not until I saw you, Dorus, head for the summer house and then when you, Anaya, said you needed time out - well, I couldn't resist sending you to the summerhouse too. And you, Anaya – you've accepted the burden – yes? Well, of course you have. You wouldn't be here otherwise."

"Yes, Ruth. I've accepted the burden and we are very happy together …."

"And did he tell you?"

"Tell me what?"

"Oh, Dorus, you are so terribly good with secrets. You didn't tell her?"

"Tell me what? For Christ's sake what is it that you two have been keeping secret from me?"

"Oh, darling. Haven't you worked it out? I was Dorus' Burden Giver. I passed the burden to him and then he passed it to you. It wasn't easy for me. You were both in such a mess, but you, Anaya, were getting it together what with going to uni. and so on, but poor Dorus was in total meltdown. So, I gave the burden to him. But look - now you've got to carry the burden after all. Use it wisely, darling."

"Dorus. You …."

"Sorry. It is the deal. Absolute anonymity. I've kept it a secret all this time just like I had to keep the identity of my client a secret. Now you know - it is such a huge relief."

Dorus' phone rang and he peeled away leaving Anaya to supply tea and cake to Ruth. The size of his smile on his return was large enough to create a temporary lull even in Ruth's exuberant soliloquy.

"That was the agent. We're thinking of selling Faulty Towers, Ruth, to fund Anaya's signature building - *Anaya's Folly*. Anyway. He says the Arab's agent wants a look. He reckons that we'll get at least one hundred and fifty mill. He's going to be here first thing in the morning for a look around."

"Wow!" Ruth and Anaya chorused.

Ruth finally ended her disquisition and departed leaving Dorus and Anaya exhausted from the volume and speed of Ruth's verbal embrace.

Dorus and Anaya found time for a quiet evening before the events of the next day were to catapult their lives into a new chapter.

*****

Saturday began with a visit from the Sheik's agent which was brief, functional and committal. A purchase price of one hundred and sixty million pounds was agreed and Dorus signed the agreement. Then, Sara Swati and her husband, Paul, arrived and after some pleasantries, Sara offered to buy the songs from Anaya for half a million pounds plus royalties. Dorus and Sara sang through the entire album whilst Anaya accepted Paul's offer of help in the kitchen. As the day came to its own conclusion about the unfolding events, the final touches were made to the dinner which was consumed, leisurely in the roof garden.

The concluding moments of the day gave way allowing Dorus and Anaya to finally climb into bed and hug each other to stop their worlds swirling around them and to re-establish their newfound mutual equilibrium.

"Well Annie. Looks like we are set."

"Yup. Here we go. This is going to be a blast."

epilogue

They absorbed London's *mise en scène* by strolling around Covent Garden and along the South Bank before eating street food at Borough Market. They then wandered the streets of London until they paused their lives and sat under the leaf mosaic of a lime tree on Hyde Park and tried to assimilate the events which had transported both of them from a world of torment, loneliness and fear to a world filled with love, happiness and hope. Their minds and their words drifted in harmony as they revisited the tides of past events.

"Dee, just think. Do you remember Ruth's party? This all began with an awkward conversation in her summer house in the pouring rain. Do you remember I nearly walked away when I first saw you?"

"Of course I remember. It seems a lifetime ago, but like only yesterday. It's crazy. I still can't get my head around how I got so involved after giving the burden to you. I had no idea what was coming. I thought giving you the burden was the end of it for me. I genuinely thought I would stop heaving the burden around and then live a sad, lonely life for the rest of my days."

"Do you think Ruth really did set us up, Dee?"

"No. I don't know. Maybe. I don't think so. Perhaps."

"Try to commit to just one answer if possible, Dee."

"Well, maybe she did. She's definitely smart enough to figure it all out for us. It just doesn't matter. The fact is, we made all the decisions from the moment we met up until now. We did this all by ourselves. Looking back on it though, I still can't believe you came back to my place after only just meeting me."

"Nor me. That was unbelievably out of character for me. Well, that definitely was Ruth's doing. I just did what she told me. I always have. I love her to bits, but to be honest, I'm a bit scared of her. But of course, she was your Burden Giver and I bet she had already worked out you would pass it on to me."

"She is a sharp cookie! Shame about her and Derek splitting up though, isn't it?"

"Is it?"

"No, not really. I suppose not. She is better off without him. He was a bit of a leach to be frank. But let's not forget it was thanks to him that my music career got launched which ultimately led to me passing the burden on to you and now, here we are. So, thank you, Derek. Wherever you are."

"It's all too crazy, but I wouldn't change any of it. For the first time in my life, I'm actually looking forward to the future. For the first time in my life, I feel I can make decisions about the things I want in my life. For the first time in my life, I feel like I don't just need to *get by*."

"Yup. It's been a rollercoaster, alright. Most of what has happened since we met hasn't been planned, though."

"No, I know. Do you think it is time we actually started to make plans? Actually start to think about our future?"

"Yes, I guess so. We need to make a plan, but can we agree that we don't actually need to stick to it? Can we keep following our desire paths?"

"Agreed. That is a deal."

"Anyway, I know what the answer is going to be, so don't bother trying. Are you going to tell me how come Ruth was carrying the burden? No, of course you won't. It's a secret, isn't it?"

"Annie. I'm not going to tell you. Because I don't know. It is Ruth's secret, not mine. All I know is that she became a world class human rights lawyer as a result. So, not only did the burden thing help get her life together, she now helps people all over the world who are suffering persecution. Not forgetting she passed it to me and then I passed it to you. It goes on and on. It's your turn now."

"How will I know who to give the burden to?"

"I have no answer. You just have to carry it. You'll know when the time comes. It's one thing you can't plan for."

"Hm. It's always on my mind."

"I know. That's why you'll know when the time comes. That's why you'll see it when it's in front of you. Just like how I saw you. But it's yours now, there is nothing I can do."

"Do you remember you had to think hard before giving it to me? Wasn't I a deserving case? After all, my life had just hit the buffers big time."

"Actually - and don't be cross, but no. I didn't have to think hard. I knew almost straight away."

"So, what was all that about going on a road trip to give me time to decide?"

"Well. I wanted you to be sure, that's all. But nothing that happened on that trip made me change my mind. I just knew."

"Well. It's all worked out well."

"I couldn't have guessed how it would pan out. I didn't guess I would become part of your journey. Just goes to show. No matter how well you plan, the journey will always offer up unexpected paths. You just have to see them."

The silence that followed left Anaya contemplative and weighed by the responsibility of the burden counterbalancing the calmness she had finally acquired in her life.

That evening they returned to the Punjabi restaurant where they spoke of their combined future which was to include completing their union with at least two children, building *Anaya's Folly* and living to the ends of their days in Cornwall in a newly reconstructed house called *Meneghiji*. They then planned their immediate future which would retrace their steps to Provence and onwards via Giverny back to the house in Cornwall which was now their home.

Two days later they headed under the Channel and drove to Provence where they sat on *le trône*, fed *la bête*, fed their bellies, fed their souls and made wishes under the shooting stars.

What was to be a brief stay revisiting the scenes that had cemented their lives together became extended when an anticyclone summoned the mistral weather system battering the cottage with winds approaching seventy miles per hour. Those nights they cuddled on the sofa wrapped in a shared duvet in front of *la bête* allowing the mildness of their voices to neutralise the brittleness of the storm. The winds swept away years of pain and gave way to newly refreshed air scented with lavender. The end of the storm cleared away the last vestiges of the hurt they had been carrying and they faced forwards to an uncertain but exciting future which they were powerless to resist but one which they had pledged to navigate together.

Their return to Cornwall was a homecoming celebrated with long periods of doing very little as they continued their journey together. The passage from being friends separated by a safety zone to being in love felt seamless but the journey from being in love to being lovers more akin to travelling an endless road. Love making opened old injuries and tested their resolve but ultimately became healing. They sought and found a serene unity by uniting their bodies.

A lazy Sunday afternoon broke the venereal tensions they still carried in their forbidden boxes when their recollections drifted back to the *Isabella* in Cannes and the free spirited, bohemian apparition who had told Dorus he must look into his Pandora's box and that Anaya held the key to open it.

"Dorus."

"Yeah."

"Is it time?"

"To open the box and look inside? There will never be a good time. Best to keep it shut and locked."

"But it is heavy, Dorus. I can feel its weight in your songs."

"I know. OK - let's do it. I've always known this moment would come. Stay with me, Annie. I don't know how this works."

"Nor me. Just shut your eyes. You always told me you can see more clearly with your eyes shut."

"OK. Hold me, Annie."

Dorus closed his eyes and shuttered out the world. His spirit floated ethereally towards a large black box. After pausing, Anaya's hand drifted into view, rested on his and they turned an invisible key together. Dorus lifted the lid and looked inside.

Returning to his corporeal self in a flash, Dorus wept uncontrollably. Anaya offered what comfort she could until his breathing allowed some discourse.

"What did you see, Dee?"

"Empty, Annie. It was empty. But the walls were stained with blood and tears."

"That's good, isn't it?"

"Yes, it's good. But can we move on now, Annie? There is another box. Your box. Can you open it?"

"I did, Dee. I already did. The night of the storm when we first made love. I opened it. It was painful, but being with you made it tolerable."

"Not empty?"

"No, but I left it open."

Have you been back to look again?"

"No."

"Do you want to?"

"No."

"Should you?"

"Yes."

Anaya shut her eyes to see, gripped Dorus' hand and peered into her box. Again, tears flowed and, as Anaya returned her consciousness to Dorus she spoke through her faltering breath.

"Not empty, Dorus. Not empty. I will have to carry what they did to me around forever. Sorry."

"Don't apologise. Maybe you will let me carry the weight with you."

"Yes. Can you?"

"As long as you let me, I will share the weight with you."

That day ended in silence but their love making before sleep was cleansing. Before the night consumed them with sleep, they reached an unspoken moment where the strands of their lives resolved in concord.

"Annie, as long as we are together; as long as we live in our safety zone together; we can carry any weight together."

"Yes, Dee. I know. The sharp pain of what happened has already gone, but the dull ache will be there forever."

"Maybe that's how it should be. We can't undo the past but we can overshadow it with our future."

Morning greeted the two time travellers who were both exhausted from their emotional journeys but who had reached a shared emotional pause. They had come to understand the task ahead and they embraced both each other and the challenge.

The days that followed consolidated their resolve and strengthened their determination. Love had become a glue to seal their wounds and the scars melded within their spiritual union. Each day brought respite from hurt and each day helped them rearrange their priorities in order to subordinate their injuries and to sublimate their desires.

An irrevocable unification signposted the way for their combined future memories.

*****

Eventually, they received notice from Cornwall Council that planning permission for the development of *Meneghiji* had been granted and Anaya immersed herself in the task of assembling a team to build their newly formed family nest. Rapidly, her time became monopolised by both the Cornish building project and by her newly ignited enthusiasm for her signature design which was to be funded by the sale of Faulty Towers. Dorus wrote more love songs and began writing an operatic work entitled *The Inspiration* describing the lives of two broken people who found love living in an emotional safety zone that they had originally constructed to keep them apart.

The sale of Faulty Towers completed with unbelievable swiftness and Anaya rose to the challenge of sourcing a suitable site to build her signature design. The design grew in sophistication and beauty following the completion of *Annie and Dee's Inspiration Tour* which included whistle stop tours to Hagia Sophia in Istanbul, the Guggenheim in New York, the Taj Mahal in Agra and the Dancing House in Prague.

Annie and Dee's Inspiration Tour, along with the rebuilding of Meneghiji and the construction of *Anaya's Folly* continued to give succour to the reconstruction of their lives and the construction of their futures.

As Anaya collected inspiration for her design, Dorus collected inspiration for his opera which was to occupy his life and become his opus magnum. Together they collected inspiration for their souls.

Rebuilding of Meneghiji began and progressed under Anaya's cynosure and eventually a building site on the Isle of Dogs in London's East End occupied by a now derelict 1970s apartment block was purchased for the construction of *Anaya's Folly*. A modestly proportioned design was submitted for approval and, following consent, building began. The demolition of the concrete block and its replacement with a transformative, futuristic structure of immeasurable beauty provided a regenerative force both for the locality and for Anaya. The design incorporated a small studio for Anaya to work in whilst in London, a small studio for Dorus to meet clients in and living accommodation sufficient for them to host guests when necessary. Most importantly, the ground floor housed an open space, designated *The Inspiration Centre*, which provided freedom for aspiring creative projects to germinate and which was funded by grants and charitable donations.

The Inspiration Centre became a reproductive ground for hitherto unidentified talent to meet and synergise. It became a breeding ground to inspire not just the incumbents, but also Anaya and Dorus. It became a space where spirits roamed freely and where suffocated souls found the courage to fly until they located their landing points.

Some years later, after the completion of *Anaya's Folly*, Anaya had been spending time working there when she stepped out into the street on a cold, snowy morning ready to begin her journey back to Cornwall where she had left Dorus working on his operatic tour de force. She was confronted by a crouched figure sheltering from the cold. Instantly Anaya found a sense of meaning. She beckoned the unknown soul into *Anaya's Folly* to shelter. Despite initial resistance but out of desperation the young lady accepted the kindness being offered. Warmth and breakfast were served whilst Anaya absorbed the story which unfolded. The name of this soul was Taome. She had been a child refugee from Syria and had been adopted by a couple in Yorkshire. They had given her the name she now carried because her birth name was unknown. After the premature death of her adoptive parents, she had established a successful café business which was forced to close after the landlord escalated the rent beyond the capacity of the café to earn sufficient funds. Once evicted, she took refuge with a man who offered shelter. There she was abused and forced into prostitution. When Anaya found her, she was not just sheltering from the bitter cold, but from the cruelty of humanity.

Anaya had known instantly. Taome was the one. Taome was to take the burden from her.

The rebuild of *Meneghiji* had proceeded in fits and starts and with the inevitable problems inherent with the application of new construction techniques being demanded of tradesmen and women encumbered with old skills. Heartaches and headaches strengthened both Dorus and Anaya. When the build was completed, it made Dorus' house into *their* family home but it screamed at the absence of progeny.

After the completion of the rebuild of *Meneghiji* and of the interior and exterior landscaping which featured a Monet style Water Lily Garden, the narrative was almost complete.

They married in a small ceremony in the newly established courtyard which was flourishing with an abundance of flowers, fruits and vegetables. The ceremony was attended by Sara Swati and Paul, Sacha and Raphaël and by Ruth accompanied by her new, female partner, Christine. As the reception took place, rain fell through the aperture in the roof and played with the water feature depicting *Saraswati*, the goddess of music and *Rati* the goddess of love. Sacha and Raphaël provided a feast of gourmet cuisine together with wines from their vineyard in Provence.

Dorus and Anaya founded a charity which they called the *Phoenix* providing trauma support in war torn zones. The UK government gave approval and consent and donated ten million pounds from overseas aide. The charity grew to encompass hundreds of trained workers supporting tens of thousands of traumatised children in war zones all over the world providing not just psychological support but a comprehensive programme of signposting of new routes to new lives away from past tragedies.

Anaya's Folly eventually won accolade from the Royal Institute of British Architects and became a template for others around the world including a grand concert hall in Los Angeles. When the Los Angeles concert hall opened, Sara Swati performed the inaugural concert as a charity event to raise money for the *Phoenix* which was now being run by Taome who had become the recipient of the burden

257

following the chance meeting with Anaya. Dorus delighted in pointing out that the acronym for the Royal Institute of British Architects was RIBA which meant to increase or exceed in Arabic and that Taome was, in fact, an acronym for 'the apple of my eye'.

Anaya used her success as an internationally renowned architect to hire and nurture new graduate architects. She paid them full salaries and gave them creative freedom to design buildings intended to change the world.

Dorus continued to write pop music and ran his own record label which he used to launch new artistes he found through *The Inspiration Centre* in London. He also invited local, Cornish singer-songwriters to record debut albums in his underground studio in Cornwall. He wrote and recorded a solo album of love songs on which Anaya played the tabla and which sold almost no copies but which they both embraced as the most important, seminal work of their lives.

As Dorus' song writing career waned, he dedicated his life to raising their two children. The first born was a daughter named Soreya who grew to be a strong woman and an accomplished cellist. In time, her musical talent expanded to incorporate orchestral and choral conducting. The second born was a son named Saul who followed in the footsteps of 'Aunty Ruth' by becoming a human rights lawyer and who defended the rights of children who had found their way to Dorus and Anaya's *Phoenix* charity.

The largest and most impressive architectural project Anaya undertook was a grand concert hall in Lahore in which the inaugural concert was a performance of Dorus' opera, *The*

Inspiration, and which was conducted by Soreya. Two attendees at that concert were Anaya's parents with whom she finally became reunited.

Dorus and Anaya's final chapter concluded when Soreya and Saul scattered their parents' ashes over the cliffs at *Meneghiji*.

Although their journey had ended, the burden continued its journey through time.